Adult Short stories
Written & Illustrated
By Peter Maddocks ©2013
Published by Peter Maddocks
And Marian Bonelli
PublishedByMe.blogspot.com

ISBN-13: 978-1481952422
ISBN-10: 1481952420

Also by Peter Maddocks
In eBook format:
Penny Crayon the prequel
Penny Crayon a Dickens of a Mess
The Sneezing Whale
Polar Bear Tales
Tick-Tock Teddy
Santa's Pipe Dream
ForgetfulNess
Sherlock Von Gnu
The Pig & Whistle of Downtrotter Farm
Bruce the Bionic Bear
Cartooning for Beginners
How to Draw Cartoons
So you want to be a Cartoonist?
Cómics para principiantes
How to Draw Cartoons
Cómo dibuja cómics
Many comic strip books
& short stories for adults

In paperback:
Santa's Pipe Dream
The Sneezing Whale
The Magic Cat Flap
Pigeon Trouble
Hot Potato
Billy Kit Car
Sherlock Von Gnu
Bruce the Bionic Bear
How to be a Cartoonist
How to Draw Cartoons
So you want to be a Cartoonist?

Many comic strip books
& short stories for adults

Index:	Page:
The Croydon Crocodiles Peter Maddocks	9
The Doorway Peter Maddocks & Marian Bonelli	33
Freefall to Hell Peter Maddocks & Marian Bonelli	57
The Grey Ghost Peter Maddocks	85
Gerhard Greenfingers Peter Maddocks	125
The Housesitters Peter Maddocks & Marian Bonelli	149
The Lakes Peter Maddocks	181
The Magician Peter Maddocks	209
The Stalker Peter Maddocks	243
Voices Peter Maddocks	277

The Croydon Crocodiles

By Peter Maddocks

Chapter One

Henry K Smith for twenty five years ran a pet shop in Croydon South London opposite a public park, that was until a couple of weeks ago when the riots broke out and gangs of youths ran amok and smashed into his shop and released most of his stock of pet animals, all this took place in the early hours of a Saturday morning. His shop was a lock up, so by the time he found out just what was going on, it was all too late, most of the damage was done by the time he arrived, having fought his way past burning buildings and streets scattered with broken glass, mobs of hooded youths carrying away the nights looted goods out of stores shattered, ransacked, windows... He then realised his business as a shopkeeper had come to an end. The door was broken in, the windows were smashed, his till had vanished and worst of all so had most of his stock. Cage doors were open and bird cages were scattered about. Inside another room his fish tanks were smashed and most of the contents were dead or dying on the floor. However worse was to come, the reptiles he kept safely locked away were missing, including a fresh water young crocodile he had recently purchased from someone whose household it had outgrown. Only the huge tank of tropical fish had been left untouched.

Chapter Two

It was now Monday morning and Henry had done his best to clear up most of the debris, but the chance of re-opening for business had gone as had most of his stock, only the tropical fish and a few loose snakes were left alive, those that hadn't died had escaped to God knows where, he had started a written report for the insurance people and the police, listing all that was missing; with the exception of the freshwater crocodile, he decided to keep that under wraps for a while, no point in creating panic, let alone a whopping great fine for keeping a dangerous animal on the premises.

He decided to look around for himself; he couldn't imagine even those hooded young thugs carrying that creature off in their sticky thieving arms. Not if they saw <u>that</u> row of teeth.

Henry having boarded up the front of the shop had managed to close and bolt the shattered front door with a lock and chain, he then went for a quiet walk in the public park opposite, the gates of the park were just across the road, where he often went and had a snack lunchtimes from the little café on the other side of the lake.

Despite the chaos of Friday night in the streets the atmosphere in the park was quite tranquil he thought, as he ordered a bacon sandwich and a large cup of tea from the café, and sat on a wooden park bench to eat his lunch and contemplate his future while overlooking the lake.

Chapter Three

He had just finished his bacon sandwich, when another elderly man sat next to him on the bench clutching a heavy walking stick with a blunt bulb like handle.
"Mind if I sit here a while?" he asked.
"It's a public park" said Henry, "please, be my guest."
The man sighed a deep sigh and banged his stick on the ground "I am so bloody angry" he said, "I could bloody well kill! I've lost everything, everything" he repeated.
"Join the club" said Henry, "were you hit by those riots?"
"Hit? I was bloody well cleaned out" he shouted, "all my stock gone!"
"You were a shop keeper?" said Henry pointing a thumb back at the roadway.
"I'm the tobacconist and newsagent on the corner" he said.
"Of course you are" said Henry, "sorry I didn't recognise you, I'm the pet shop."
"Bloody hell!" said the man with the stick holding his hand out, I'm George Greenaway."
"And I'm Henry K Smith" replied Henry taking his hand, "terrible business" he said.
"Terrible, it's that bloody block of council flats behind us" said George, "even folk who live there are frightened to go out at night."

"Its youth unemployment" said Henry, "it's getting worse."

"Youth unemployment my arse!" said George waving his stick, "thieving bastards more like! I know what I would do with them, National Service, that would sort the thieving yobs out, either that or bang 'em up for good. I've lost everything, God knows it was difficult enough trying to run a business let alone rioting and thuggery, I even had to hide my tobacco and cigarettes so the bloody customers couldn't see them! Health and bloody safety didn't stop the yobs from finding them though! Did you lose much?" he asked.

"I did, and I don't know what to do about it" said Henry, "half my stock must be running around this park…"

Chapter Four

"Oh my God!" he said out loud, and stood up looking at the lake!

"What's wrong?" said George.

"There could be a problem with this park lake," he said, "a <u>real</u> problem!"
"What kind of bloody problem?" said George, "it's us that's got the problem, not that bloody lake!"

"It could be a <u>very</u> bloody lake if one of my animals has gone in for a swim" said Henry.
"Animal?" said George, "what kind of animal?"
"An animal with a large row of hungry teeth" said Henry, "an Australian fresh water crocodile" he said quietly.
George let out a long low whistle, "and you think it's in that lake?" he said pointing…
"I'm almost sure of it" said Henry. "Nobody carried it off; of that I am certain, and this lake is just perfect for that monster!"
"Monster?" said George, "how big is it?"
"Big enough to do a lot of damage to anyone getting within grabbing distance, he hasn't been fed since last Thursday, not by me, anyway!" said Henry, "I had better report it."
"Hang on" said George, putting his heavy walking stick on his shoulder, "Keep schtum about this! It could be useful!"

"How do you mean useful?" said Henry, "how can a man eating crocodile be useful…?"

"Exactly!" said George, "let me make a few enquires."

"I don't follow you" said Henry, "that croc, if he is in that lake he is fucking dangerous! Not fucking useful!"

"Just you wait and see" said George, taking a mobile phone from his pocket, "I'll show you how useful!"

George talked on his mobile with his head turned away and a hand over the phone as if in total secret conversation. Henry walked over to the edge of the lake and looked for any sign of a ripple on the surface.

"Right!" shouted George, "can you meet me here tomorrow, around…" he looked at his wristwatch, "one thirty, lunchtime, yes?"

"What else have I got to do?" said Henry shrugging his shoulders.

"Good man" said George getting up and waving his heavy walking stick. "Until tomorrow then" and off he went!

Chapter Five

Next day Henry opened up his broken shop doorway, and once more checked what animals he had remaining alive inside, he fed and watered what he could and decided he would have to get shot of all that was left and close down for good, meanwhile outside, the local M.P. was wandering from broken door, to broken door promising that all the culprits would eventually be caught and brought to justice. This Henry K Smith knew was total bullshit, as the politics' of the area was now so confused that you could not tell one from the other, only the far right seemed to be gathering any strength from the diabolical actions of the weekend – people at street level were very angry, nobody in the area felt safe anymore. Henry ignored the political chanting of the local M.P. crossed the road and walked through the park gates. It was almost lunchtime.

He arrived at the park café to see George Greenaway already sitting on the bench; he gave Henry a greeting wave with his heavy walking stick.
"Can I get you a coffee?" said Henry.
George raised a pint mug of beer and smiled, "get your coffee and come and sit down" said George, "we need to talk."

Henry sipped his coffee, it was hot; he sat down and nodded a 'hello' at George.

"Now then" said George, banging his heavy walking stick on the ground. "Let's get to business! You recon this monster croc of yours has made his home in this here lake?" he said, pointing his stick.

"Certain of it" said Henry, having another go at his piping hot coffee, "where else would a freshwater crocodile go, other than in a freshwater lake?"

"Exactly!" said George, "where else! Now I've made a few phone calls to those who have been smashed up or robbed in our community, we agree on one thing – revenge! We are going to teach these yobs a lesson they will never forget. Now, have you got any other water creatures with teeth?"

"I've got a tank full of piranha in the back room" he said, "they have all got teeth."

"Fantastic!" said George "couldn't be better."

"Now come on!" said Henry, "you are not suggesting we release piranha fish into that bloody lake?"

"Too right I am cobber" he said, "keep that Aussie croc company."

"I'm not sure they would survive in fresh water" said Henry.

"Isn't that Amazon fresh water?" said George, "been a few years since I was at school, but I think I'm right."

"Now, how the hell am I going to get a tank full of piranha fish down here?" said Henry, "they are nasty viscous little creatures, at the best of times."

"Wonderful" said George, "leave all the worrying to me, I have friends in low places" he said tapping the side of his nose… He then turned his back to Henry, and sitting on the far end of the bench he made a very private, very secret phone call. "Okay" he said, turning around flicking his phone shut with one hand and pushing himself up on to his feet with the aid of his club head walking stick.

"All arranged, two men in a van will collect your fish around eleven tomorrow morning, I will be here to receive them, so don't worry they will be safe."

"I'm not worried about the fish" said Henry, "just be careful, they are nasty, vicious little creatures."

"Great!" said George banging his stick on the ground, "vicious, nasty, angry is just what we want!" he then shaded his eyes with his hand and scanned the lake… "Any sign of your Aussie crocodile yet?"

"No" said Henry walking to the water's edge, "he could be anywhere, the hedges, or the undergrowth."

"Nah!" said George, "if I know anything about crocs, they love the water, he is in the lake! I'd put money on it."

"I hope so" said Henry, "at least we could then contain him."

"He's our ace in the hole" said George.

"I'm off, I've got an insurance man due at four" he said looking at his watch, "I've got to make a list of my stock that's missing before I get the visit" said Henry.

"Say nothing about that crocodile" said George pointing his stick at the lake, "or those piranha fish, "we need those to get our own back on those thieving yobs."

Before locking up the wreck of his shop for the night, Henry checked what was left of his remaining stock, two rabbits [having escaped the loose snakes], six kittens and fifty four piranha fish, they would be collected by two men in a van in the morning, he fed the kittens and the rabbits, but George had told him not to feed the piranha fish – 'keep 'em hungry' he had said!

Chapter Six

Next morning on time, the van arrived and two men, both young, arrived each carrying a net and a large bucket with a lid spattered with small holes. They set to work having filled their buckets with fresh water, and transferred the snapping fish one at a time from tank to bucket, they both wore strong gloves to protect from losing a finger or two from those razor-sharp teeth.

He told them they were pygocentrus nattereri, known as the red bellied piranha that could strip a hand of fingers in seconds, freshwater fish…
"But they may not survive cold British lake water" said Henry.
"Let us worry about that" they said, "George has a plan and it doesn't include the lake!" They emptied his tank of fish, and those now in the two buckets were kicking up a racket; as they carried them to the van it was like carrying buckets of boiling bubbling water!

The fish were not only hungry they were disturbed, and tightly packed together in a confined space.
"Angry little buggers" said the driver, "are you getting in or walking across?" he said.
"I'll walk over to the park and join you after I've locked this wreck up" said Henry as he picked up a hefty lock and chain across the front door.

"Not that I've got anything left for those bastards to steal" he shouted as the van pulled away…

As Henry arrived at the parks café, George was busy in the bushes opposite the café instructing the two young men where to deposit the buckets of fish. Henry brushed aside the bushes and joined George who was busy pointing his heavy walking stick and shouting instructions.
"You are not putting them into the lake?" said Henry.
"No need" he said, "we will tell a few porkies about the lake when it comes to piranha, I just hope that croc of yours shows up when we need him, that lake is just a bit too cold for your monsters!" he said pointing to the two buckets, "they sound bloody angry, just listen to them!"
"They *are* hungry" said Henry, "not been fed for two or three days!"
"Perfect" said George, "just what we need, hungry, angry, gnashing razor sharp teeth!" he then turned to the two young men, who were drinking cups of tea from the café in the park.
"They've just arrived" shouted one of them, "they are just parking the van."
"Good" said George, "have they got the merchandise?"
"Yeah!" said the other young man raising his cup of tea in the air, "no problem!"

Chapter Seven

The merchandise turned out to be three male teenagers, two white and one black, all with their hands tied behind their backs with a plastic strap, the kind you can't release unless you cut them loose. They were being escorted by two strapping men with arms like legs of mutton tattooed from wrist to neck, their necks decorated with gold medallion's, heads shaved clean and glistening in the sunlight!

"Bring them into the bushes" George shouted, pointing.
The teenager's started to shout and swear threatening us with their human rights...
"You've got no human fucking rights here!" said one of the brutes cuffing one across the back of the head so hard he fell headlong into the bushes!
"Now then lads!" shouted George, "this is a game of question time – like the one you lot have <u>never</u> seen on television. The game is simple, we ask the questions, and you give us answers – understood?"
"Fuck you!" said the one with a haircut like a Red Indian, again, he also was cuffed around the back of the head, he then turned and lashed out with his feet, only to receive a face full of fist that struck him to the ground.

"Question time!" shouted George, "I want names and the addresses of the yobs that looted my shop, the tobacconist on the corner back there" he said, bending down to the one on the ground who was bleeding from the nose...
"Fuck you!" the youth answered!

"Right, let me explain something that might change your point of view" said George pointing at Henry, "the same yobs from your little gang robbed and looted this gentleman – now he owns that pet shop a few doors down from my tobacconist, but he has things that bite! Not things that make you cough, like mine. He has nasty vicious creatures not unlike you lot! But unfortunately you turned them loose to wander the park. Out there in that lake" he said pointing with his fingers spread open "is a large Australian freshwater crocodile swimming happily around the lake, and by now, tired of eating fish the size of a finger on your hand. Now..." he said prodding the lad in the stomach, "now he is looking for meat, he hasn't been fed meat since you lot set him loose! And you young man, would make a fine meat meal!"
"You're just bluffing" said the youth, "I see no crocodile!"
"That's just it" said George, "you never do see it, until it's too late and you are being dragged beneath the water to drown, before he starts to rip you into little pieces. I tell you what – we will

chuck your mate in first, the fat one" he said pointing him out, "and you can watch – do you think that would loosen your tongue?"

Henry steps in and says "you can't do that George! It's my croc and we could all be done for murder!"

"Well my business has been ruined by this scum" says George, "and I've got nothing to live for, I wouldn't mind a rent free comfortable cell with everything found; I hear they have a good library, they've closed ours in the town!"

The two remaining youths said they knew the culprits, but thought we were just bluffing...

"There is no Australian croc!"

"I assure you there is!" said Henry.

Chapter Eight

Let us try something that I think will definitely change your young minds" says George, "in those two buckets we have a large group of piranha fish, just in case your lack of education has failed to inform you of such a creature, I will demonstrate, first we remove the lid, and as you can see, it is stocked full of small fish. Now watch closely as I drop this chicken carcass into the bucket."

As the meat hits the water all hell breaks loose in the large bucket, a black swarm moves over the carcass making the water seemingly boil – then within a few seconds, calms back down leaving a chicken skeleton remains with not an ounce of flesh left!
"Impressive!" said George, "very impressive, did you like that?" he said to the leader of the group, the youth said nothing, not even an expletive!

"Now what if I lifted the lid of this one here" said George, "and our two strong friends here lifted you up, turned you round, we don't want you to *see* your hands being eaten, tied together as they are, and plunge those meaty fingers into our fish filled water tub."
The two powerful men lifted the yob and slowly lowered his hand into the water, while George dropped food into the other bucket making the piranha noisily disturb the water.

The youth let out a scream along with Henry and the two other lads…

"We'll tell, we'll tell you names and addresses" they shouted.

"Is that blood or water?" shouted Henry as they lifted the youth upright.

"Water" said George, "no blood!"

The other two distressed lads; were led away to the café to give names and addresses…

"You can stop screaming now" George said, "your hands are all in one piece, that bucket is just full of water" then pointing, "that one is full of flesh eating fish."

"You bastard!" sobbed the youth.

"Cut him free" said George, "we've got what we wanted,"

As the tattooed man arrived waving a piece of paper "We've got seven names" he said, "and four addresses."

"That's a start" said George, then pointing at the youth squatting on the ground looking at his hands, "take him to the café and get him a hot drink to calm his shattered nerves, which is a damned sight more than his kind did for us!"

Henry said "you scared the living daylights out of me – I could have sworn those other two mates of yours filled both buckets full of my fish…"

"They did" said George, "but these are tubs not buckets, we emptied the fish into that tub, and just filled this one with water, we're crafty bastards, not barbarians!"

"What are you going to do with that list?" asked Henry.
"We show it to that local M.P. and he will see nothing but <u>votes</u>, then we go to the police and watch as they pick up that scum who wrecked our shops! Revenge!" he shouted, "an eye for an eye!"

Chapter Nine

We all had a stiff drink at the café then sat outside in the sunshine on the bench, the three youths were set free and went off calling us names with threats! George made a phone call and said that M.P. would meet us at the café here in the park at four o'clock this afternoon, so we agreed to turn up for the meeting at four.

Henry went and had a fish and chip lunch, it being a Friday while George had copies of name and addresses printed to hand out. At four o'clock as arranged they met the M.P. at the café in the park.

He was pleased to be handed the names and addresses of the culprits, but said he first of all would need proof that they had the right thugs who smashed up their businesses, and not just anybody.

Henry and George sat listening to his doubts when they were confronted by a group of lads with a pit bull terrier, straining at the leash they were holding and showing a mouthful of saliva covered teeth...
"We smashed your fucking shops!" they shouted, "and now it's your fucking turn!"

And they let go the lead as the pit bull lunged at George...

Henry grabbed George's heavy walking stick and hurled it into the lake, the pit bull could not resist the challenge, it chased after the air born stick and leaped into the lake as it entered the water, everyone turned to watch the dog swim towards where the stick had fallen, when suddenly, a long jaw full of teeth followed by the body of a crocodile lunged at the swimming pit bull, and dragged it beneath the water by its head held firmly in its jaws! And then... nothing! Both had vanished!

"Well!" said George, "there's your crocodile, anyone want to join him?" he said as two tattooed men came out of the café.
The M.P. said "I'll call the police" as he dialled on his mobile, "they need to be informed about this and the list of names and addresses of you lot!" he shouted as the yobs turned and ran...
"I've already phoned the local newspaper" said George, "they love the idea of Croydon having its very own crocodile!"

The End

The Doorway

By Peter Maddocks

Chapter 1

Jack Stevens was always good with his hands, he was never an academic, but give him a set of tools and a box of wires, plugs and electrical bits and he was in a world of his own. Something always would come out of his tinkering something you or I had never seen before. He held down a very good job working for a company that made television sets, or at the very least put them together from components that arrived from the Far East. Jack enjoyed his work at the factory and was well liked as a workman who knew his job and could be trusted to guarantee the end product when completed. The money was good, but above all, he was happy day to day, working in an environment he liked and a job he found both interesting and helpful, with his hobby playing around with electrics.

Don't expect me to describe exactly what he did as a hobby because I'm a man who writes books, and I still have trouble changing an electric plug. All I know about Jack is exactly what happened to him as a result of him messing around with electricity and his digital knowledge with electrical pieces or bits.

It all started on a Friday with an earth shattering statement made by the parent company back in the Far East.

They were closing down production in their English factory as from ten days' time; redundancies will be paid according to time served and years of service. So read the statement pinned on the notice board on the factory wall.

Jack was a young single man with no ties, although he still had to pay his rent. Harold the manager was well liked, and a man who would listen to what anyone had to say, however, this decision was final, so all anything anybody had to say had to include – goodbye! Jack did get to ask if with his redundancy money he could purchase some of the components now surplus to requirements, lying about in boxes. Harold, who himself was being dumped after some thirty years of dedicated service, had told him just help yourself Jack and hang on to every penny of your redundancy money, you are going to need it.

So help yourself, Jack did, taking home various bits and pieces over the next ten days until the shutters came down and the factory closed for good. Jack decided to spend two weeks on his hobby to try and complete the job before going out into the world of job hunting…

As far as I can make out, Jack was a great fan of action movies, big wide screens, like those we see when watching cinemascope movies of yesteryear.

The screen he had built was wide, about seven or eight feet and two foot deep mounted across an old dining table. It was during one night, he was woken by a loud crashing sound, and he leapt out of his bed and ran into his 'hobby room', the huge screen was up ended leaning against the wall looking like a doorway.

The thin table legs had given way on one end, tipping or I should say, upending the television screen to lean against the wall. Jack checked the frame to find it was all together in one piece, and as far as he could see nothing apart from the table legs was broken.

However he was now up and awake so he went back into this bedroom and put on his slippers and his dressing gown and then switched on all the lights to make sure there was no broken glass about. All seemed to be fine so he moved the broken table away from his upturned television screen and removed the broken legs. And swept the splintered wood away from the wall, then leaving the broom against the screen while he removed the debris, he then turned to find the broom handle had vanished… it had somehow dropped into the television screen. The brush end was on the floor at his feet, but the handle was nowhere to be seen, bending down to pick up the broom end he pulled it towards him and the handle re appeared, it was still complete, the

37

handle was still fixed to the broom head, how was this possible thought Jack. The broom had fallen into the screen. He put the flat of his hand out to feel the glass – his hand melted into the screen, it was no longer solid, Jack stepped back to see his reflection in what should have been glass, there was no reflection. Then he fell forward, catching his foot against the bottom end of the upturned screen throwing his body forward into the frame, he had tripped out of his slipper on his right foot and was now face down on the floor, he looked up to see he was now in a very large, half lit room, or studio, yes it looked like a studio. He saw a television camera to his right, and there was another one on his left. There was a television monitor in front of him; he had visited such a place many times as an electrician, delivering components from the factory. He stood upright, he looked down at himself, he was still in his pyjamas and dressing gown and yes, one slipper was missing, and his right foot was bare. Behind him, he could see nothing, no sign of his room or his television frame leaning against his wall. He rubbed his head with both hands he rubbed his face, shook his head, no he was not dreaming, he was not asleep. This was real, but how?

He walked around the studio, there was a splendid red settee, a large low table, that he almost fell over, huge television arc lights here, there and everywhere, it was a very genuine television studio. The type you would see when they read the news from the monitor in the morning while you sat eating your cereal. Then from the far end of the studio, there was a shaft of light, someone was coming, a door slammed and he heard voices, he had to get out of there.

Jack Stevens had to find his way out, and quickly, there were more lights switched on and he could now see everything between these two cameras, he thought this is where I came in; he hobbled over with his one slipper and walked slam bang into a solid wall. He held his head and looked down, there was the other slipper, the wrong way round the toe pointing towards him, he quickly bent down and found himself able to lean forward and pick it up, and he turned his head to see he was now half into his own hobby room, he quickly stepped forward…

Yes he was back in his own environment, he looked behind him to see the large upturned frame of his screen leaning against his wall, he was out, it was no longer a television screen it was a doorway. A three dimensional doorway. Jack Stevens had unknowingly invented, <u>accidently</u> invented a doorway of the fourth dimension – Magic!

What time is it? He rushed into his small kitchen to look at the clock on the wall six thirty, 'the news' he said, 'I must switch my TV on in the bedroom.' Jack went to his television where he watched late night films from his bed, plugged it in and turned it on. It was as he thought the early morning news and weather, the screen lit up and a talking head appeared, and then as the camera pulled back, there were the red settee and the low table, it was just as he had seen only this time is was occupied with newscasters. He, Jack Stevens had his own personal doorway into the television news studio, fantastic! 'I'm a television hacker' he shouted, he danced around the room shouting 'I'm a television hacker! I'm a television hacker!'

Chapter 2

He ate his breakfast cereal sitting on the end of his bed watching the news on television; he studied every camera move, mentally taking note of the furniture around the set. He couldn't wait to try out the doorway again; he must get dressed and work out what to do once he got back on the TV studio set. He must learn to blend in, he had visited television studios quite a few times when he worked at the factory and he knew once you were in and past the usual security checks you were left alone to wander about. He of course with his doorway could bypass security checks, so he should be free to look around. He went back into this hobby room and stood looking at the frame leaning against the wall, then, taking a deep breath, he stepped into the frame.

His doorway into television, it worked, he passed through easily, smoothly, having placed a spare shoe on the floor of his hobby room pointing into the frame, this he hoped would show him the way back. All he had to do is walk up to the studio wall and look for the shoe, fingers crossed. Once in, he must now try not to look conspicuous, he must blend in, he saw a clip board on top of a camera as he entered, and he picked it off the camera and moved out of the studio and into the alleyways around the various sets.

Then he arrived at the canteen and tucking the clip board under his arm he ordered a coffee and sat down at a table and surveyed the scene.

Here and there he saw a known television face, but the canteen was mainly full of studio workers. A very attractive young woman suddenly appeared carrying a coffee and a donut on a plate…
"Is that seat taken?" she said.
Jack said "no, help yourself. Shall I take that hot coffee off you before you drop it?"
"Oh thanks" she said, "it's my first day and I'm as nervous as hell."
Jack starred at her face, she had the most beautiful green eyes, not too much make up and even teeth as white as snow – she was beautiful, her hair was auburn and tied back off her face, she had an educated London voice. Jack couldn't take his eyes off her as she chatted away nervously.
"I've yet to find out who I'm supposed to report to" she said.
"Who are you with?" asked Jack.
"The newsroom… research. I've got a name, but I can't find her" she said taking a bite of her donut.
"Would you like me to help" he said holding out his hand, "I'm Jack."
"Hello Jack!" she said wiping her hand on a tissue before shaking hands.

Jack held her hand and felt a rush as he did so.

"If you could point me in the right direction" she said, "what do you do?"

"Oh" said Jack pointing "I'm... I'm with the camera crew..."

"Great" she said "lots of cameras everywhere!"

"That's a fact" answered Jack. "What's your name, just in case I have to introduce you" he said hastily.

"Kate" she said "Kate Wyatt, W-Y-A-T-T, with two T's" she spelt out.

"Okay Kate. Newsroom you said"

"Yes, research" she answered.

"I'll take you there, have you got to pay for coffee?" he said standing up.

"No" said Kate, "don't be silly, you pay when you get served at the till."

"Of course" said Jack, "stupid me, so I did!" he moved away from the table.

"Your clipboard" said Kate pointing.

"Oh heck yes! I'll need that" he said.

"Are you sure you work here?" said Kate with a grin.

"Of course I work here, what makes you say that" said Jack.

"You seem more nervous than I am" she said.

It's <u>you</u> Kate, <u>you</u> make me nervous, you're so beautiful.

Kate gave him a playful push. "Come on, find me this Newsroom" she said.

They both eventually found the Newsroom and Kate took out a piece of paper from her shoulder bag, "Dorothy Medowes" she said.
"Well this is the newsroom, they must know where this Dorothy woman is" Jack said, eyeing a security man watching them both.
Kate waved the piece of paper in his direction and the security man joined them.
Jack stepped back "I must be going Kate, I'll see you again, good luck!"
"Yes thanks, see you" she said, and then started talking to the security man showing him the paper in her hand.

Jack turned and moved away, he had to get clear of the man from security in case he asked questions, time he made an exit. Jack moved around the studio looking for the place he came in, it was between the two cameras, but they were in use and moving about, he was about to start looking for the shoe when camera two swung around and the cameraman said to Jack "are you maintenance?"
"Yes" lied Jack.
"Shift those cables" he said, "there's something affecting this bloody camera."

"Leave it to me" said Jack putting down his clip board, and he gathered the cables and separated them, the cameraman signalled a thumbs up, and Jack returned the signal. He then went back to pick up his clip board from against the wall – and there on the floor was his shoe pointing in his direction! He checked he was not being watched and bent down picking up the shoe and took a step forward, melting into the wall. He was back into his hobby room, he was out! And totally clear of the newsroom!

Chapter Three

He went into his bedroom and flopped onto the bed with relief that he had escaped detection and that he had met the beautiful Kate, what an adventure he thought, I must see her again.

He decided to take a shower, freshen up, he studied himself in the bathroom mirror, not bad looking, medium height, good teeth, dark brown hair, one small problem, he had no class, and he had the common touch. Whereas Kate had class, great looks, classy voice, she had that walk that women from her class have, a beautiful confident knowing walk. 'I'm in love' he said to himself, not before time, I'm already going on twenty eight. Next time I go through that door, I'll look good and smell good. Smart jeans, clean shirt, hair washed, make an effort Jack! Impress her, show her you care…

He went through his meagre wardrobe and smelt every shirt he came across. He found a book that reminded him of his beloved dead mother, a book of sign language. She was born deaf, and him being her only child she had taught him how to sign. Bless her, he thought, ten years since his mother had died and still he missed her, he signed, I love you Mum! into the mirror…

First thing he must now remember before he entered the doorway, was to leave a shoe pointing inwards, twice it had got him to his exit, so this, he must always do! And this time he said picking up a football boot, I'll leave you, couldn't be more conspicuous when I look for it to let me out, my lovely red football boot. I hope the clipboard is where I left it? By the side of my 'Doorway', it made me look official, someone of authority, I'll use it again!

He was ready, all spruced up looking good, he lifted and sniffed under both arms, and smelling good – fresh! He studied himself once more in the mirror, not bad, not bad at all he said to himself, now where's that red football boot…

He placed the boot at the foot of the 'Doorway' pointing inwards, and then with a deep intake of breath, he stepped into the frame. He quickly turned to his right, yes, there's the clipboard… then he melted into the television studio.

It was busy, people everywhere, the two cameras were moving around aiming at their subject. Men with sound booms moved about the floor, arc lights were hot – Jack walked slowly around the studio, silently, stopping occasionally, as the cameras moved from subject to subject. No one troubled him; he even got a knowing nod from the sound boom men as if he was part of the crew.

He moved out of the studio and down the alley of cables to the door marked newsroom, it was open, so he looked in. A middle aged woman was sitting at a desk and looked straight at him without saying a word, but she had 'what do <u>you</u> want?' written all over her face.

Jack changed his clipboard from hand to hand, and said "Kate, the new girl?"
The woman lowered her eyes and just pointed with her pen, Kate was at the far end of the room talking to a colleague, she caught sight of Jack and gave a slight wave, and Jack mouthed *"everything okay?"* And she raised a thumb and continued her conversation with her colleague. Not to push his luck, particularly as the woman at the desk had her eyes on him again, but now with that 'we all know she is pretty' look!

Jack who now felt embarrassed turned and left, he must be satisfied that Kate had acknowledged him, with a half-smile, he thought, enough to keep him going today. He must wait until he can get her on her own, in the canteen maybe?

He was suddenly brought back to reality when someone said "are you an electrician?"
"Yes I am" said Jack with confidence.
"We're having trouble with the arc lights in studio four" he said "follow me."

This he did, and entered studio four to be met by a studio audience! A couple of hundred grey haired people, who were all sitting in rows facing a stage full of actors and actresses standing about.
"There are two arc lights above giving us lots of trouble" he said. *He* was obviously the stage manager.
"Okay" Jack said "I'll see to it, leave it to me…"
"Good man" said the stage manager and marched off to address the audience.
Jack sorted through the cables and the wall boxes and eventually found the fault and corrected it in record time, much to the applause of the floor manager and the actors – a job well done!

Jack suddenly felt good about himself, it had given him confidence, and he no longer felt he was an intruder.

Lunch time came and he went to the canteen with the hope of seeing Kate. He sat at the same table as he did before where he first met Kate – Wyatt, with two T's! Almost an hour past and Jack was just about to give up when he saw her, she was just getting lunch on a tray and she waved at him and joined him at the table.
"How are things going with the new job?" Jack asked, taking the tray from her hands.
"Just great, its early days as yet, but everyone is so helpful" she said as she sat down.

Jack thought, as he gazed at her, she really was the most beautiful woman in the room, and he was sitting talking to her.

"You look very smart Jack" she said.

My goodness! She remembered my name he thought. "I have a meeting this afternoon" he lied.

"I've got to nip out after I've finished this" she said, "I've got to collect some scripts from across the road."

"I'll come with you" said Jack "I've got another hour or so before I'm due back."

"Okay" said Kate "let's do that! Just let me finish my lunch and we'll go."

Jack felt good, things were going well, that electrical job had given him a new confidence, and now he was with the lovely beautiful Kate…

Chapter Four

They left the canteen together and walked to the exit. Jack could see all the traffic through the huge glass windows as they approached the main doors of the television studio.
"We have to pick up our badges so that we can get back in, we get them from the desk over there" said Kate pointing.
Jack stopped, official badges! You have to give your name and they look you up on their computer! A cold sweat came over Jack.
"Oops!" he shouted putting his cupped hand to his ear, "phone!" he said turning away, "Okay" he shouted, "sorry Kate, they want me back in the studio right away" he lied.
"Okay, no problem" she said and went to the desk to sort out her badge.
Jack waved to her as she left, cursing himself for his stupidity, off course I can't come and go as I please I'm a loose cannon around here. He went back upstairs watching Kate cross the busy road at the crossing through the window as he climbed the stairs to the news studio. Better call it a day, he thought, before I make any more stupid mistakes. I'll see Kate tomorrow, I'll ask her out, take her to dinner in the evening, and we could go and see a show of her choosing. I haven't touched my redundancy money; I could really treat her like she should be treated, with class!

So right now he would make his exit and arrange everything for tomorrow evening. He entered the news studio looking down at his clipboard as if he was about to do something, and slowly made his way around the walls stepping over camera cables to the back wall of the studio where he last made his exit, between the two cameras, he passed the first camera and stared with horror at the second one! There on top of the camera was a red football boot…

The cameraman suddenly appeared and seeing Jack said "hello mate, come to check out the cables again? Had no trouble with this next show, and a good thing too as we have a full studio team with guests. Hey, looking at the football boot are you?" he said, lifting it off the camera, "God knows whose it is, who loses one red football boot?"
Jack could hardly speak "w-w-where did you find it?" he stuttered.
"Over there" said the cameraman pointing, "up against that wall, one red football boot, it beats me! Who loses one boot? Is it yours?"
"No" said Jack, then thinking quickly, "I'll take it to lost property, maybe someone knows something."
"Well let's face it" joked the cameraman, "you would notice a one legged footballer almost immediately, wouldn't you!" he laughed.
Jack tried to laugh back, but his mouth was too dry.

"Here you are then, good luck!" said the cameraman handing him the solitary boot.

Jack took the boot and moved back against the wall hoping it would swallow him up while he was clutching the boot. No such luck, the wall was solid, all the way around – Jack had lost his exit…His slipper and then boot must have in some way been keeping his dimensional door open! He is going to have to chance his luck at the main entrance somehow, and get back home that way! He made his way to the front exit, the same as he had done with Kate, he stopped at the top of the steps looking down on the exit floor, and there was the desk where you ask for your badge. There were three officials on the desk and two security guards on the door, checking all who came in and all who went out, pretty well impossible to make a break for it. The only chance he had was the desk, bluff it through, a terrible risk, but there it was, if he wanted to get out of the building that's what he had to risk, being found out as an unwelcome intruder. Once more, he had to take a deep breath and take a chance; at least Kate wasn't going to witness his humiliation.

Once at the desk he asked for a badge, through a very dry mouth and sweaty palms. He gave his name at the desk, Jack Stevens, silence as the desk clerk went on the computer.

"Yes Mr Stevens, we've been awaiting your arrival" the clerk banged a bell with his hand and called over a security guard saying "take Mr Stevens up to the news room studio, he is expected."

Jack froze "there must be some mistake" he said, "I was asking for an exit badge?"

"The computer says you are to be taken to the news room studio sir. Those are my instructions. Have you any baggage sir? Apart from your clip board and – ahem!" he coughed, "your football boot!"

And with that the guard grabbed Jacks arm and led him back up the stairs. He was taken to the news studio and left to fend for himself, Jack waited, then made his way to the canteen and bought a cup of coffee and a donut, and sat trying to work out just what had happened…

Chapter Five

He sat with his head in his hands for almost an hour, he definitely could not get back to his hobby room the way he came in, the boot which acted as a key to his exit was here with him on the <u>wrong</u> side. The only other way for him to get home was via the front exit, but they wheeled him back in, instead of out, he must try again.

Once more he approached the desk for the television studio exit. "Can I help you" asked the very same desk clerk.
"Yes, I need an exit badge please" said Jack in a bold voice.
"Name" he said going to his computer.
"Jack Stevens" he almost shouted.
The desk clerk looked up from the computer and said "Yes Mr Stevens, we've been awaiting your arrival" and he banged the desk bell and called over the same security guard saying "take Mr Stevens up to the news room studio, he is expected."
"No!" shouted Jack "I want an exit badge – now!"
The clerk again calmly said "the computer says you are to be taken to the news room." Again the security guard grabs his arm firmly and marches him back up the stairs and leaves him outside the news room studio.

My God! Jack said to himself, it's just like groundhog day, I can't leave, I'm imprisoned in a television studio, I can't even get thrown out! I'm trapped in here forever like a goldfish in a glass bowl...

He sees Kate in the canteen every day, and she keeps him up to date on her many trips to the theatre and dinner dates with her various boyfriends. Jack can only sit and look at her lovely face and listen to her tales, he can NEVER ask her out...because he can NEVER get out.

Jack is popular as an electrician, a news room assistant, an assistant cameraman and general maintenance; he gets well fed because he also works in the canteen. His clothes? Well the wardrobe department have everything he needs too!

And dear reader should you be a light sleeper or suffer from insomnia, you can always watch Jack Stevens in person on television as he translates late night films in sign language for the deaf.

The End

Freefall to Hell
By Peter Maddocks

Chapter One

My name is Jack Weston, I am twenty six years old and I'm strapped for cash, broke! I owe three weeks rent on a so called, one bedroom, third floor apartment in Purley, south London, and I can no longer dodge the landlady, she is after my blood [and cash!]

I have just been told by the guy who works in the local post office, that there is a temporary job going, and its cash in hand! All it is, is flying an advertising balloon, so more like a days' entertainment than work, and apart from holding a full commercial pilot's license, I also have experience at flying gliders from Kenley airport. So would I be interested in such a job? I most certainly would! I had said. He gave me details and a phone number to apply, and this I promptly did.

The morning of the trip was a beautiful one. It was just gone 7am when I arrived at the chosen site, clear skies, a light wind, perfect for hot air ballooning, I was; they had told me, to be accompanied by a qualified balloonist, who would assist me to raise this monster into the sky, unfortunately for me though, the balloonist known as Henry, who was supposed to be my co-pilot, had been heavily on the booze the night before, and although he had turned up, said, he was far too hung over to fly, but he was here to assist me in take-off, and in releasing the anchor ropes; but not until he had run through the basics of balloon flight with me! He would also be part of the retrieval crew, who will track the balloon on the ground.

So here I am, in the middle of a field near Godstone in Surrey, looking up at a huge air balloon disguised as a can of soup, with a huge basket and a couple of gas cylinders to get me far afield, the gas jet beneath the envelope of the balloon, fitted to send hot air up into the balloon, to raise it off the ground and high into the clear blue yonder! I couldn't wait; I had my mobile phone with me to take photos of the views, which should be awesome on such a beautiful day…

We were amongst about 15 other hot air balloons, most were the normal kind, which was good for us, we wanted ours to stand out from the crowd, and our banner will be unique! All the teams were in good spirits, and the day bode well.

It took nearly an hour to fill our huge advertising balloon, which was now ready for take-off. Henry reminded me to throw out the advertising banner, which was rolled up at the bottom of the basket, when I reached a thousand feet.

They will be looking to see that banner! Henry said, it's important, the whole purpose of the flight! No banner, no wages!

The cast off went smoothly, the flame from the gas jet was doing its job, by filling the monster with hot air, the weather was indeed perfect for flying, a cloudless blue sky, the gentle breeze, I felt I was almost going to enjoy this job today, and it was going to get my rent paid! And of course having a head for heights, flying gliders, I had no fear of motor-less air travel. I looked down at Henry hangover, waving from the field below.

The balloon climbed steadily to a thousand feet above the ground, registered on the dial fitted to the gas cylinder, time to throw out that important banner. I first made sure that the rope attached to the banner, was securely strapped on to the side of the basket, it wasn't easy to anchor it there, I had to take off my gloves and my fingers were cold. I needed to get it set right, because Henry told me earlier, 'as you drift, you will tow the outstretched banner for anyone below to read with ease.' The banner at the bottom of the basket was heavy canvas, I had spent a good amount of time with it between my feet, so I had a struggle lifting it, especially as it had twisted and turned as I had done, but eventually I pushed it over the side.

The heap dropped like a heavy lead weight towards the ground, snapping to such a halt on the attached line, that it tipped the basket, throwing me headlong, I would have been saved, had I not become entangled in the banner itself…. Then for a moment time stopped as I could see myself suspended on the wrong side of the basket, and with a sudden jolt I was thrown headlong out into space… Rapidly I went into free fall still with the banner attached to my leg, as I plunged down to the earth as a helpless wreck… Above me the ridiculous huge can of soup balloon collapsed as if squeezed by a giant hand and followed me down.

Chapter Two

I have no recollection of what happened next, except for the fact that I was lying on my back, looking up at the sky. Was I alive? Or was I dead? A question I could not answer, as although I could see the sky, I couldn't feel my legs or my arms, I could <u>not</u> move a muscle. But I could smell onions!

I managed to turn my head, and my eyes were looking at two green wellington boots, attached to bare legs and then, looking up I saw a young woman in an apron! With a round face, green staring eyes, with long brown hair surrounding her head like a halo.

She was looking down at me. "Are you in pain?" she asked.
"No" I said, "I can feel nothing, I can't move anything – but I think I'm alive!"
She then knelt down beside me and squeezed my hand, "can you feel that?" she said.
"I can feel nothing!" I said. "My whole body is numb." She squeezed my legs, and pinched my nose! "Nothing!" I repeated. "But I can smell onions?"
"That's because you are lying on my onions, in my vegetable patch" she said, "I'm going to leave you for a moment, and I'll be back."

"Can you get help?" I asked her... I don't know if she heard me or not, but she didn't answer. I tried desperately to move a leg, or an arm, even clench a fist, but I could move nothing. I could hear very little of my surroundings, no birds, just a sound of wind in nearby trees, grey clouds overhead were moving in, building up over where I lay. With all I could have worried about, I wondered if I was going to get rained upon now too! And then I was aware she had returned, with a wheelbarrow.

"I must get you inside my cottage, and make you comfortable" she said, "it's going to be a struggle, but I'm going to lift you into this wheelbarrow."

"No!" I said. "You must get help, you can't lift my weight!"

"There is no chance of help" she said, "don't worry, I am very strong." And she put her hands under my armpits, and lifted me up with ease, dumping my torso into her wheelbarrow, and then she grabbed my feet and lifted my legs...

"How did you manage that?" I said, as she lifted the handles of the barrow and wheeled me down a garden path. I could smell rotting plants, unsure if they were in the barrow with me, or in the raised flower beds we were passing by.

Chapter Three

"Have you phoned for an ambulance?" I said.
"Don't have a phone" she said blankly.
"I've got a mobile phone!" I said, it must be somewhere, it was in my jacket pocket when I fell, if must be here! Where is the banner I came down with? *And* where is my jacket?"
"They landed in the fire, I was burning… things."
"How could the banner *and* my jacket be in the fire? That doesn't make sense…"
"Forget about them." She said dismissively, she turned the wheelbarrow around to pull it up the front doorstep, of what I could now see was a thatched cottage; she wheeled me inside, and kicked the front door closed with the heel of her foot.

Apologising to her again, for the havoc I was causing, I then mumbled to myself bang goes my rent money!
"I'm going to put you in my box room to rest" she said, "there's a comfortable bed in there, and then I will make us both a cup of strong tea." She banged the side of the doorway as she dragged me and the wheelbarrow into the small room, alongside a single bed; it looked like one of those old-fashioned metal hospital beds from the History Channel!

She had to climb over the bed, first kicking off her boots, to get down in position to lift me by the shoulders onto the bed, as she bent to make the lift, her mass of hair brushed my face, I could see it, and smell it, she smelled of blackberries in August, a strong heady pungent smell, odd though, it being April? The thought past through my mind, as she unceremoniously clambered back over the bed again, grabbing my ankles and straightening me out, like a lump of meat on the bed! Then she just left me; she dragged the wheelbarrow back out of the doorway, turned and closed the door.

Chapter Four

Alone, I looked around at what I could see, just a bare white wall to my right, and to my left an empty bedside table, there was just a small leaded cottage window opposite the bed, through which I could see very little, due to the plants and debris outside! Everything else in this room was white and barren.

The young woman returned, still minus the boots, she had kicked them off climbing over the bed, but she was carrying a large mug that she put down on the bedside table, with five or six straws.
"What's your name?" I said. "Mine is Jack, Jack Weston."
"My name is Carmela" she answered, putting a straw into the mug of whatever it was."
"Carmela what?" I asked.
"Just Carmela" she repeated as she put her hand under my head, and lifted it so that I could get the straw into my mouth, "drink" she told me, "it's cooled down, its tea, and it will moisten your mouth."
I drank from the straw, but could taste nothing, then trying to catch what breath I had, I said, "you must try and get some help, get a doctor, or better still, an ambulance, to take me to hospital for treatment."
"I know what I am doing" she said, "I'm a trained nurse, you are in capable hands."

"You live alone here" I said, "no family, no husband?"

"Just me" she answered, "I am in good, safe hands… and so are you!"

"Well, at least I have accommodation!" I said sarcastically, "this accident has blown my budget, blown the chance of me paying my rent debt; I've nowhere else to go."

"Exactly" she said, standing up, "now, you rest for a while, that tea of mine should help. I will go and change, then I will come back and tidy you up." And once more, she left, this time leaving the door open.

I tried hard to hear any kind of movement outside, is there a road or a motorway? But I could hear nothing, not even a bird was singing, all I had was silence in that white room. I wasn't cold, I wasn't warm, I wasn't anything, but my mind was clear…

Chapter Five

Time passed, and Carmela suddenly appeared, "right!" she said, "we must get you cleaned up, first we must get those clothes off, your trousers are torn, and your shirt is hanging from your bones, she unbuttoned what there was left of it, and physically ripped it off my body without moving me, then removing my shoes, correction shoe! God knows where the other one was! Off came my socks, then moving swiftly, she unbuttoned and unzipped my flies, I tried to object, but could do nothing to restrain her! And then she tugged off my pants, pulling from the trouser cuffs, exposing me in nothing but my underpants, the final item to come off! I was naked, everything exposed to those starring green eyes of Carmela's, and she again left the room, but returned almost immediately with a bowl of steaming water, and a large sponge.

"I'm going to wash you down" she said, "I want you to call out if you feel anything, this water is warm, but not hot." She commenced by sponging my face, then each arm – nothing – then my chest, and my legs, - nothing – she returned the sponge into the bowl and soaked both her hands for a moment, then she handled my genitals, fisting my penis, it went rigid, "this is a very good sign" she said smiling, and commenced rubbing it up and down!

I almost swallowed my tongue, "what the hell!" I shouted…
"Can you feel this?" she said looking straight at me, continuing to masturbate me.
"I can feel nothing but embarrassment" I shouted.
"It means the blood is getting to your genitals, this should give you hope" she said, and loosed her grip on me, picking up a wet sponge and washing that area clean, but by now my penis was rock hard, "you said you felt nothing in that area?" she said.
I lied, "of <u>course</u> I could feel it, but I can't do anything about it, every other part of my body is numb!"
"I'm going to get you more tea" she said, picking up the bowl and sponge, "at least you are now clean…"
"And I'm embarrassed!" I shouted at her.
"I told you, I'm a trained nurse" she said, as she left the room.
"Since when does a trained nurse start masturbating a totally disabled man?" I said, my words going unheard, and I looked down at myself lying naked in a strange house on a strange bed, with a <u>very</u> strange woman looking after me in a very strange way…

I realised I hadn't eaten since God knows when, yet I wasn't hungry, and how long did I lie looking up at the sky? Time has passed, yet it's still daylight outside, as I gazed at the leaded window.

I could still feel no movement in my arms or my legs; I could just about make a fist with my hands now, or was that just in my imagination? My God! I thought, am I now paralysed for the rest of my life? Here I am in this crazy young woman's bed, one who lives alone, and I can't move a muscle. I must convince her to make contact with somebody on the outside world, and get me help! And as I thought, I drifted into a dreamless sleep…

Chapter Six

I was suddenly woken to find Carmela, naked, and astride me! Bouncing up and down on my rigid penis in total ecstasy! I could not move, only lay there like a log as she writhed and twisted... I found my voice at last; I think I was too shocked at first to speak. "What's going on? What the hell do you think you're doing? Hey Hey!! Can you hear me woman?"

Nothing, she was lost in passion, but physically very much here and now! She continued to bounce on my body, her arms either side of me giving her support, her beautiful breasts bouncing up and down with her, before my face, then she leaned back, arching her body and crying out, as we both reached a climax... I felt a rush flow from my rigid penis into her body – there was no pleasure in this activity for me, no desire, no passion, just a simple bodily function; she was breathing heavily, her head down, and her long brown hair covering her face, then suddenly she dismounted me, as she would a horse. And stark naked, she left the room, she said nothing...and what more could I say? I had been used for a purpose.

Carmela returned with a bowl of warm water, and a large sponge. She was now dressed and wore a white apron, then without saying a word she began to sponge me down again, from head to foot, paying particular attention to my genitals…
"I'm going to give you another cup of tea," then looking at the bedside table "she said. "Have you used up all your straws?"
"Fuck tea!" I swore. "What I need is some kind of explanation, of what the hell you think you are doing!"
"I would have thought that was quite obvious" she said, still sponging me down, "don't tell me you have never had sex before?"
"Not while I was totally incapacitated, and without me being able to join in!" I said, "bloody hell girl, I am a sick man here, I am crippled!"
"You are not sick, I can assure you" she said, "your mind, and fortunately your bits are working fine."
"Not to <u>my</u> fucking advantage they are not…" I shouted.
"No need to shout Jack" she said, "I am not deaf."
"Listen" I said. "For all <u>your</u> sexual antics, I felt nothing, zilch! Not even a rush, we just exchanged fluids."
"Exactly" she said, "I'll go and get your tea now, and some fresh straws." She picked up the bowl and sponge, as she once more left the room.

Chapter Seven

Leaving me washed clean, humiliated, still naked, and motionless, looking up at a blank white ceiling…

I noticed after a time, there was no light fitting hanging from the ceiling. I turned my head and looked at the bedside table, no sign of a light, no wall lights either, and no sign of a light switch.

Carmela returned, with a mug of what she called hot tea, plus a handful of straws for me to suck it through. I had no sense of taste, and I still hadn't eaten and had no hunger pains. I had very few feelings at all, I could see, thank God I could hear, but that was it, nothing else.

"When does it get dark" I asked her, as if nothing else had happened.
"It doesn't" she replied.
"How can it <u>not</u> get dark?" I said. "What time is it?"
"Forget all these stupid questions and drink *that* tea" she said.
"Are you sure this is tea?" I replied, "I can't taste a thing."
"It will keep your mouth moist" she said, "I will want more sex from you later!" she shouted as she left the room, she stopped, taking a piece of paper out of her apron pocket… she stood studying it.

While I shouted what time is dinner time, when do we eat? "Are you hungry?" she said looking back. "No, I am not hungry" I mumbled.
"Then you have no need to eat" she replied, then placing the piece of paper back into her pocket, she counted something out on her fingers and left the room.

I shouted after her that she could forget sex and get me some help – not bloody sex – that's meant to include two people enjoying each other, not one bouncing up and down taking advantage, "do you hear me!" I screamed, "I'm not your bloody slave to do as you will! Are you listening?"

Chapter Eight

This small box room was my prison, my God, I thought, I'm a sex slave, you read about such things going on in tabloid newspapers, but you never ever believed they were true!

However, Carmela returned naked, she did have a glorious female figure, still in the blossom of youth, her long brown hair rested on her shoulders and down her back, her round face set off her green eyes, that looked straight through you, not at you, with that long, long stare, with her mind ticking over in deep thought... Then she was on me, this time she handled my penis working it to its full length and then wrapped her mouth around it to make it moist, so that it entered her easily, as she straddled my body. Then again, taking the weight with one arm either side of me she worked up into a frenzy of passion on my penis, I could do nothing but watch her perform on me, and then she leaned back, her arms raised above her head, lost somewhere to herself and me, those wonderful breasts moving unhindered, her face and chest flushed, she seemed to bloom before my very eyes... Yet I lay there, feeling nothing, no satisfaction, no feeling of elation, nothing.

I could only watch her pleasure herself on me, watch her head roll, and her hair flaying the air as she bounced and moved, backwards and forwards in deliberate movements to accept all that was inside her, and once more, her timing for the final rush of us reaching an orgasm together was perfection, and, as I filled her with my sperm, she screamed a great shout of fulfilment as if she knew…

"I think we scored that time!" she said, as she left my rigid horizontal body.

I lay there, with a feeling of self-disgust, a useless heap of a man unable to participate in anyway shape or form, I was a prisoner, where was the '**we**,' when she said **WE** scored?

Chapter Nine

Later, Carmela returned, dressed, carrying that bowl of steaming water, and that fucking sponge…

"I'll clean you up and you can rest" she said, as she sponged me down, yet again, "I won't be bothering you again, I am now **pregnant!**"

"Shouldn't you have asked my permission first" I said, "a man should have a say in the sexual act, let alone one to produce a child, I don't even know your full name" I added.

"Nothing unusual in that" said Carmela sarcastically.

"I have a right to know what is going on!" I said.

"You have no say on anything anymore" she said, "so just keep quiet; I'm going to bring you another cup of tea…"

"I don't want your lousy tea, I can't taste it, it could be poison for all I know!" I yelled.

"No need for poison" she said smiling, "just embalming fluid, completely tasteless! I called it tea to get you to drink it!"

"Bitch" I said, no didn't just say it, I shouted it, aimed at the small window… hoping someone, anyone, other than her with the bloody sponge, could hear me.

"Don't shout" she said, plonking that sponge into that bloody bowl, "nobody will hear you, nobody will <u>ever</u> hear you.

You Jack Weston, will <u>never</u> reach twenty seven, your life was terminated by that fall, you are DEAD. You were dead when I found you, you were dead when I brought you in, and you are dead **now**."

"Don't talk rubbish" I shouted. "You are fucking mad! You've just raped me, how do you rape a dead man? Tell me that you stupid woman. I need help, I'm not dead, I'm sick, now get the fuck out of here, and get me help, you've had your fun, now let me get out of here and away from you – you crazy cow!" I tried every muscle in my body to make me move as I ranted and raved at her, but it was hopeless, I really was paralysed. I tried to calm down, "Carmela" I said, looking up into those starring green eyes, "please, put me back into that wheelbarrow of yours, wheel me out of this place and leave me so that someone can find me and get me help. I won't say a word about what has happened, or who you are, or all that sexual activity, I'll say nothing, it never happened, I just had the balloon accident, and fell out of the sky."

"You are dead, Jack Weston, no one can help, once you go out of that white picket gate of mine, you will crumble to dust, as would I, should I try to leave this place. I am a witch; I am in the hands of the Devil, ordered to produce a son for him, your son, the one we have just created."

"You really *are* a mad woman" I said, "I am dead you say, you are also dead! And <u>we</u> have just conceived a son for the Devil… Crazy bloody woman, just get me out of here! Now!" I screamed as loud as I could, she just ignored me, and left the room, closing the door to this prison, this bloody fucking mad house, I screamed another great scream again, but nobody came, nobody heard me.

Chapter Ten

I lay, entombed in that room the door was closed, for all I knew it was locked. Carmela never came back again, I was left helpless, never being hungry, never feeling thirsty, just helpless – a living death, with just my eyes, my hearing and my thoughts, no sense of time passing, my body was always intact, I had no bodily functions it seemed to worry about, even that raped penis never reacted again!

Months, even years, must have passed with me locked or shut away in this room, many years... Many, many years!

Until one day, the door opened, it was a woman, Carmela, older, with longer, wilder hair, and harder, more mature features, but still with those starring green eyes, that looked through you, never at you, Jack, I've brought someone to see you, Jack Weston," she said, pushing forward a boy of thirteen or fourteen, "this is Damien, my son. He is now fifteen years old, a fine young man, and a credit to us all" she repeated.
"Who is us?" I said.
"Never you mind who, he will take charge one day, The Master has assured me so."

I looked the boy up and down best I could from my still horizontal position, "so this is my son" I said.

"Dead people do not have sons" said Carmela, "they just produce, as we have done. We have no claim on him."

The boy said nothing, turned, and left the room.

"Why the viewing?" I said. "And why show him to me now?"

"He, the boy, requested it" said Carmela, "it's all part of his training, he must know everything, there must be no doubt in our society, we do not believe, <u>we know</u>! We all must know! Everything! The Devil master commands it!"

"And me? What happens to me in this great plan of yours" I said.

"You and I" she said, "have played our part in producing a fine son for our master."

"Not my master" I said. "You can keep him!"

"The Devil is in all of us" she said. "You can never ignore that fact! All those religious wars, it's the Devils work – **Your** God has nothing to do with it… Take a long hard look at religion, and think again Jack. However, it is wheelbarrow time for you and I Jack Weston, you get your wish, as you are about to leave this place, both you and I, together…"

And she put both arms under me and lifted me off that bed, as if I was a small child in his mothers' arms, and she carried me out into that perpetual daylight, and placed me in that wheelbarrow I had travelled in so many years ago.

Carmela again lifted the handles, and pushed me down the garden path to the white picket gate… She stopped and unbolted the gate, she propped it open with a large stone.

"Are you going to leave me outside, in this contraption to be collected?" I said astonished!

"No" she answered, "we go out together, you once asked, why is was always daylight here, that's because in *their* world, out there…" pointing past the gate, "there is *always* darkness, we witches serve our master, the Devil, in *their* darkness – my work is done. I have produced a son, Damien, for the master, who will share their world and do great things in His name. But, you and I could be nothing but a burden to him, so we must go."

Chapter Eleven

So, she took the handles of the wheelbarrow, and walked out into the darkness, and in doing so, both turned to dust, no trace that Carmela and Jack had ever existed…

Many years later, a mature man with a brilliant reputation in both politics and religious studies, was recruited as an advisor and confidante to the Archbishop of Canterbury.

His name was: Professor Damian Weston!

The End

The Grey Ghost

By Peter Maddocks

Chapter One

My name is James Bradshaw; I am seventeen years old and have been at sea for two years. The year is nineteen forty six and I am about to join the Grey Ghost in Southampton, as a third class passenger, on route to New York, U.S.A. I am to join a ship called The Silver Coin.

The Grey Ghost as it is known in merchant navy circles is The Queen Mary, painted grey as she had been carrying troops to Egypt. Now, she is about to return to being what she was built for, a passenger ship; 766 cabin class, 784 tourist and 579 third class, that includes me!

She is big, 975 x 118 feet, weighing 80,750 tons, a monster of the seas capable of doing 35 knots plus. She holds the blue ribbon for crossing the Atlantic in three days, twenty hours and forty two minutes.

I was carrying my belongings in a kit-bag slung over my shoulder as I arrived, overwhelmed at the size of her, compared to the ten thousand ton Norwegian tanker, which was my last ship – amazing!

I went on board and showed my papers and was directed to my cabin in the third class section of this huge ship.

It was like Piccadilly Circus on board, all kinds of people coming and going in every direction. After a walk that lasted at least twenty minutes, I was led into my cabin only too pleased to drop my kit-bag off my shoulder. Cabin number one three seven, looks comfortable I thought.
"Which bunk is mine?" I said, relieved to get the weight off my back.
"The top one son" came the answer, from a man about forty five, smoking a large cigar, "my name is Winthropp. Two P's... John Winthropp, I'm heading home after four years of Europe."
"James Bradshaw" I said, "going to New York to join a ship."
"So I've got a real sailor in my cabin then" he said, "that's why you've got the top bunk son, I've got a gammy leg, a war wounded man without a purple heart medal – government service. No uniform. What time does she cast off? Do you know, being a sailor boy?"
"Sometime this evening" I said, "not sure of the exact time. Has she got many passengers?"
"I saw a gang of excited young women coming aboard this morning" said John Winthropp with two P's, "G.I. brides somebody said, going to join their G.I. husbands, scattered all over the U.S.A. I'm off to find a bar, I need a drink, and this leg of mine is giving me hell. Will you join me?"
"I don't drink sir" I said.
"How old are you son?" said Winthropp rubbing his leg.

"I'm seventeen" I answered, "Eighteen in April."
"Well that's a good thing, not to drink" he said, "kills your liver, besides stateside you can't drink till you're 21 - You've got a long thirsty wait" he said, taking a silver headed walking stick from off the lower bunk, "come on, I'll introduce you to coca cola" he added.

We left our cabin and headed out into the alleyways in search of a bar, once on the upper decks there was much activity, lots of people coming and going fore and aft, in search of whatever or whoever they were looking for. We found a very posh bar and ordered our drinks from the barman, in a smart white shirt and black waistcoat, and wearing a bow tie, bright red! I had never seen a bow tie before, I couldn't take my eyes of it, and we found a table and sat down. The bar was buzzing with people all very excited at what was going on. Lots of activity everywhere as The Grey Ghost prepared to leave Southampton.

We sat listening to the girls chattering amongst themselves in their excitable way, I had never seen so many young women, even though I did have seven aunties, who visited on and off as I had grown up in Birmingham. My mother came from a large family of seven sisters, and four brothers. They, the brothers, were Royal Navy, whereas me, I was Merchant Navy.

Thank goodness it means that I could join or leave a ship whenever and wherever I wanted, and didn't have to follow orders.

Hours passed, and I walked around the ship for what seemed like miles, God she was big! Then suddenly I was aware of her throbbing engines under my feet, Parsons geared turbines were alive, driving quadruple screws, we were on the move! Small ships were sounding their horns wishing us a safe journey, the ships decks were alive with crowds of people waving to the other mass of people on the quayside, some seventy or eighty feet below us. Huge ropes and cables were coming aboard, as we edged ourselves away from the dockside, no matter how many times I have done this aboard ship; it is always a thrill of the beginning of a new adventure…

Chapter Two

We were now under way, her massive bow cutting through the Atlantic waters like a razor sharp knife through cheese. A soft warm breeze disturbed my brylcreemed hair as I ventured forward and surveyed the lifeboats, big enough to each carry fifty or sixty people at a push, I reckoned each one seemed to be the size of a fishing trawler.

I felt good, I was leaving land and doing what I always wanted to do, go out to sea and visit other lands, other countries, always on the move from port to port. And now here I was, heading out on The Queen Mary, The Grey Ghost.

I slept well the first night in that top bunk, the cabin was small, but well equipped, with a mirror, a sink, a lavatory, a table that pulled out, and the door out to the alleyways. We didn't have a porthole so we must be in the centre of the great ship. John Winthropp snored a bit, but was good company in the waking hours.

Next morning I jumped down out of my bunk as quietly as I could, so as not to disturb John who was still sound asleep. I washed my face, used the toilet, cleaned my teeth and hastily dressed so that I could go out on deck and get some air.

There was much activity on my deck – mainly white coated waiters, and catering staff preparing for the breakfast hours work. I could still see land at the stern of us, it must Ireland I thought, once we lose sight of that, it's the open waters of the Atlantic day and night until we reach Halifax, Nova Scotia, our first port of call.

I looked over the side, amazed at the speed, the Queen of the seas was well named, and she just moved that sea aside as a knife would open an envelope. God, she was fast!

I found a restaurant, where I could get a light breakfast of tea, toast and marmalade, and <u>real</u> butter. People started to join me, and eventually filled the restaurant with excitable chatter. The wonderful smell of bacon and eggs reached my nostrils, and I was told to go help myself, all I had to do was pick up a tray and a plate, then fill it with piping hot food. All this was a first for me, not having to turn my hands to a day's work to earn my tucker, fantastic!

I was half way through, enjoying my fantastic breakfast, when I was aware I was being watched; two young women were looking at me from the next table. When they saw that I was aware of them, they both waved – not the kind of 'hello, how are you' wave – more like the kind of wave

you would give a child, a kind of *Yoo Hoo!* Wave, wriggling their fingers...
"You're enjoying that my love" shouted the one with dyed blonde hair, "that breakfast" she said, "have you never had bacon and eggs before?"
I shook my head, "not for years" I said. "My dad used to have it before the war!"
The second young woman, with long dark hair and bright red lips said "you enjoy it, my lovely, plenty more where that came from. Growing lad like you needs a good breakfast. Are you with your parent's?"
"No!" I said reluctantly, "I'm a Merchant Seaman!"
"What?" they said both getting up and pulling up chairs to sit opposite me, "you're a bit young to be a sailor boy!"
"I'm eighteen" I said in a stern voice, "well eighteen in April" I corrected.
"Fancy!" said the blonde, "Elsie and I are G.I. brides, going to join our husbands in New York. Pity we are married women ain't it Elsie, we would love to have a handsome young sailor like you!"
"Yes" said the dark haired one, "especially one who's just discovered bacon and eggs."

We all laughed at that one – even though I was a little embarrassed.
"Have you got a girlfriend" said the blonde, leaning forward.
"No" I said, "I haven't."

"Have you *ever* had a girlfriend?" said Elsie.
"No, not ever" I answered reaching for my mug of tea.
"Not only a sailor boy" said Elsie, "a <u>virgin</u> sailor boy! Now, there's a rare thing for you" she said. "How long have we got before we reach New York?"
"Three or four days" I said, "but I don't know how long we dock in Halifax Nova Scotia for, so it could be five or even six days."
"Never mind," said the blonde one "gives us plenty of time for us to make a man of you!"
"Oh yes!" said Elsie, "we can't have you going ashore in New York a virgin. There must be laws about that!" And they both got up from the table laughing, "one of us will sort you out and it's me first!" said the blonde, and she blew me a kiss with her hand…
"Kate" said Elsie, "you know very well *I* saw him first!" And with that, they both gave me a proper wave and left the restaurant, to go out on deck.

I went back to my cabin to see if my fellow passenger John had got up yet.

He had, and was shaving in the mirror "hello lad" he said, "where have you been?"
"I just had my breakfast."
"What did you have?" asked John.
"Bacon and eggs, *and* was joined by two very flighty women!" I boasted.

"Really?" said John. "Now be careful lad" he said stroking the razor down his neck, "some of those women I saw coming aboard are a bit more than flighty!"

"But they are only joking" I said, "they are married women; they told me so, both going to join their husbands in New York."

"That may be so" said John wiping shaving soap from his face, "but love for some of 'em was far from their crafty minds when they signed that marriage certificate, what they saw my friend, was a ticket out of war torn Europe and an American passport!"

"No!" I said, "these were two nice fun loving women enjoying themselves."

"If you say so son" said John, "all I'm saying is just you *be* careful."

"I will" I said. "Aren't you going to have breakfast?"

"I've had my breakfast" he answered waving a hip flask.

"I'm going to explore this glorious ship" I said.

Chapter Three

And I went back up on deck, people were now huddled together on deck chairs, which made me smile, as they were on the wrong side of the ship, you must always sit on the lee side, unless there is a head on wind or gale, then you stay below. There was now quite a strong cold wind blowing, I should have put a jacket on, so I headed across to the lee side out of the wind, and on arrival noticed there was quite a swell, the mighty ship was starting to roll a bit. Groups of people were holding on to each other as The Grey Ghost rolled into the swell, the passengers, unlike the crew were having difficulty keeping their feet on the deck, and boy, did she creak with each roll! I was told she had no stabilizers, quite surprising for such a big ship. I looked over the side and waited, first we were ten or fifteen feet from sea level, and then, as she lurched to starboard she was eighty or ninety feet from sea level. God! She could roll! I could hear the groups of girlie screams with each movement, even the male passengers hung on for dear life, as they saw a deck chair or two make their way to the railings unaided! Crew started to appear on deck making things fast, and folding the deck chairs away.

"We're in for some heavy weather" said a deckhand as he past me, "best go below" he said.

"I'm okay" I said, "I'm used to rough seas; I was on small tankers that would bob up and down like a cork in a bathtub!"
"In that case" said the deck hand, "give a hand and get the passengers below. If it gets any rougher even these decks could be awash, the wind is getting up!"

I edged my way along the deck and saw a young woman clinging to a deck rail for dear life! She looked terrified. I got to her and said that we should go below.

"I'm not moving" she said gripping the rail with her knuckles white, "I can't move; I'll fall over."
"Here" I said, "let me help you."
"If I let go of this rail, we'll both slide down the deck" she cried.
"Hang on to me instead of that rail and we'll make for that doorway…" I said pointing. "Come on, give me your hand."

She did just that, and we managed to edge our way along, each time waiting for the roll to starboard, until we got to the doorway. I looked back at the horizon, "I think she's changing course" I said "turning into the wind, and that should make it easier, more comfortable."
"I didn't think a big ship like The Queen Mary would bounce around like this" said the young woman, as we staggered along the passageway.

"No matter how big the ship" I said, "the mighty sea will bounce anything when it gets angry. Here's the restaurant, shall we have a drink?" I said.
It was almost empty, "just water for me, I couldn't keep anything else down" said the girl.

We both sat at a table, and I ordered a coke and a glass of water from the bar. "You see" I said, "she a lot steadier now, changed course!"
"Thank goodness" she said taking the glass of water from the barman with both hands.
"Is this your first trip?" I asked her.
"Yes, my guardian is taking me to New York, to join my parents. I've been at school in London."
"School?" I said, "How old are you?"
"Seventeen" she said, "How old are you?"
"Same – eighteen in April" I said, "but I left school at fourteen, I've been at sea nearly three years."
"Oh I see" she said, "You are a member of the crew?"
"No, I'm a passenger, like you, but I am a seaman, I'm joining a ship in New York. I'm James Bradshaw by the way, what's your name?"
"Marian, as I said, I'm with my guardian."
"Where is he?" I asked.
"It's a she..." she laughed, "being sea sick in the cabin, she looks green!"
"Poor woman, I've never been sea sick" I boasted, "never!"

"I must find my way back to my cabin" said Marian, "she, Mrs Campanella, will be worried…"
"That's if she's got her head out of the sink!" I joked, "come on, we'll find your way back together."

The boat was a lot steadier now, so people were coming out of their cabins and filling the alleyways –
Suddenly a voice said "you didn't waste any time sailor boy!" It was the blonde haired Kate, followed by Elsie, the dark one.
"Hello" I said, "just helping Marian to find her cabin."
"Naughty boy!" they laughed – "Are you taking her to see the movie this evening? It's the latest film, Brief Encounter!" said Kate! "A bit like what you two are up to!"

I was getting embarrassed, so I just waved and moved on…
"You know those two women?" said Marian looking back.
"They sat at my breakfast table" I said, "I don't <u>know</u> them!"
"I should think not" said Marian, "a couple of tarts!"
"That's a bit strong" I said. "They are two married women going to join their husbands."
"G.I. brides!" said Marian, then, "we're here, cabin two seven two, this is mine."

99

"Would you like to go to see that film?" I said, "that's if we can find the cinema."

"You will have to introduce yourself to my guardian first" said Marian, "but yes, call for me here at seven thirty; I think that film starts at eight o'clock."

"You knew about the film then?" I said.

"Yes, of course, haven't you got an itinerary?" she said.

"A what?" I said.

"A program telling you what's on, and where" she said. "You're a passenger, you should have one."

"I'll check when I get back, and I'll be here [looking up], at cabin two seven two, at seven thirty sharp!" I said.

"I look forward to it!" the girl smiled and went into her cabin.

Chapter Four

When I got back to my cabin, John Winthropp with two P's, was sitting at the small table writing, "where did you get to?" he said without looking up.
"I was on deck" I said. "It was a bit rough up there!"
"Bit rough down here" said John, "the steward popped his head in to say we could be heading for bad weather, the forecast isn't good, he told me not to leave anything loose hanging about the cabin."
"I'm off on a date tonight" I said.
"You're not hanging about with those two women?" said John turning to face me.
"No, of course I'm not!" I said, "I met a young girl in distress, being bounced about on deck during that swell!"
"I see" said John, turning back to his writing, "good for you, but keep well away from those other two. The steward tells me they are on the game."
"Game?" I said. "What game?"
"Good God son, you are wet behind the ears – prostitution! – They are two known prostitutes on the game! Now, have I spelled it out for you?"
"But they are married, and going to join their husbands in New York?" I said.
"Not if *they* can help it!" said John.

"They? Who are they?" I said, "and where did you get this prostitute information from?"

"The steward" said John. "They know a prozzy when they see one. Now…" he said, with a wave, "go away and let me get on with this letter, I need to get this on its way tonight. Oh! Pass me my stick, there's a good lad."

I picked up his stick from the cabin floor, and was surprised at how heavy it was – and hung it on the back of his chair.

"Thanks" he said, "I want to get this message to the wireless room tonight, and I'll need that stick! Particularly if that weather forecast is anything to go by. That steward said we are in for a real blow!"

I spruced myself up best that I could from my kit-bag, most of it creased, but it was clean. I had used the local laundry before I packed, however, I was presentable. I'm ready to show myself at cabin two seven two, at seven thirty for inspection by Marian's guardian, fingers crossed! I said to myself, as I closed my cabin door.

Chapter Five

The Grey Ghost was bouncing around a bit by the time I got to cabin two seven two, I knocked on the door and cleared my throat as I waited for it to open. Marian appeared smiling and looking beautiful, she asked me in with her finger to her mouth and a shush! Evidently the guardian had taken to her bunk with a box of tissues and a bucket!
"Its okay" said Marian, "she knows I'm just going to the cinema, she is in no mood for anything else, come on let's go."
"It's hot in this cabin – it's no wonder she feels seasick!" I said quietly as we left, and closed the cabin door.

The cinema was quite luxurious considering what the ship had been through. We had two very comfortable seats with a good view of the screen. Pathé news was just starting, showing the latest troubles in Palestine and the Middle East. Then came the film, Brief Encounter starring Trevor Howard, I thought it was going to be a western! But it turned out to be what I thought was a dull love story, of two middle aged toffs! However, Marian thoroughly enjoyed it; she even shed a tear at the end! People applauded and two women were introduced live on stage as British Film stars, one was Ann Todd, and the other ladies name was

Phyllis Calvert, said to be on their way to Hollywood. Whatever, it was a good night out, so I suggested we go to the restaurant for something to eat. Marian agreed, although she said she wasn't very hungry, but would enjoy a cola. We found a seat easily, as the ship was still bouncing about a bit and we passed quite a few people in the corridors, looking a bit green around the gills! I ordered a couple of cola's, and there were dishes of what looked like nuts and crisps, with another which was full of large green oily peas, Marian told me they were olives. So we sat and nibbled and drank our colas, talking about the film we had just seen.

When suddenly blonde Kate appeared and sat at our table. "Have you seen Elsie?" she asked.
"The dark haired Elsie woman, that was with you?" I said.
"Yes!" she said angrily, "<u>That</u> Elsie, have you seen her?"
"No, we…" I pointed to Marian, who was looking a bit annoyed, "…we've just come out of the cinema. Why, have you lost her?" [Stupid question], but I wanted Kate to move on.
"She was supposed to meet me in the bar, two hours ago, but there is no sign of her, anywhere. As you know, we share a cabin."
"No, I didn't know that" I said, looking at the reaction on Marian's face.

"Well we do, and I haven't seen her since eleven o'clock this morning. She had a meeting at twelve with some bloke, and now I haven't seen her since!" she said.

"Do you know this *blokes* name?" I asked.

"Don't be bloody silly" she said, writing on a piece of paper with a pen from a fringed handbag. That's our cabin number, if you see her, or hear about her, come and tell me. I'm worried, bloody worried, she is always in contact with me – always." And with that, Kate got up and left, leaving me with a piece of paper and a rather cross Marian.

"Good thing my guardian stayed in her cabin" she said. "You would have lost brownie points talking to that one, while you are sitting with me."

"I didn't have much choice did I?" I said, putting the piece of paper in my pocket, "she sat herself down uninvited."

"Come on" said Marian, "I had better get back to *my* cabin."

I paid for the drinks, and we made our way back along the corridors. The ship now was really beginning to rock and roll about, "shall we take a look on deck before you go in?" I said, as we got to cabin two seven two.

"Not really" said Marian, "I should show myself, it's getting late." She squeezed my hand and said, "thank you for a nice evening" and went into her cabin.

Chapter Six

I turned away to go up on deck, when the cabin door opened again, it was Marian with a handkerchief over her face, "Oh God!" she said, "it smells of vomit in there! I really think I *do* need some air."

"Come on then" I said, "let's go up on deck." So hand in hand, and with a big smile on my face, Marian and I went up on deck for air, and air we got! It was not the lee side, and the wind was gusting and wet, so we hurried around to the protected side out of the wind and rain. That's if it was rain, more like sea water coming off the top of huge waves. The Grey Ghost was really bouncing about, and creaking from every bolthole. The lifeboats were banging about, straining on their davits as the Queen hit an oncoming wave. I was enjoying every minute, particularly as Marian was clinging onto me for dear life.

I said, "let's go up, close to the funnel in the centre; the view of the angry sea will be fantastic from up there!" We were still on the lee side, protected from the wind, so it was easy going, we climbed the steps up onto the top deck, and stood huddled together, close to the bulkhead at the foot of the giant centre funnel.

The view of the seas was fantastic, wild and angry, rocking The Grey Ghost as she ploughed on cutting through any mighty wave it could muster. She was at war with the North Atlantic!

We were so excited, the noise of the sea, wind, and the engines of the Queen made us cling together, and turning, I took Marian in my arms, I kissed her, and she kissed me back, then we both laughed, here we were alone on the deck of The Queen Mary, in a wild storm, somewhere in the North Atlantic. "You will always remember this" I said. "Every time you see a picture of the Queen, that we kissed by the centre funnel, late at night in a storm in the Atlantic."
"It is late" said Marian, "I must get back to the cabin."
"Okay" I said, "I'll go first, you stay close behind me, the steps are steep and very wet."

As we got to the lower deck on the weather side, it was awash with sea water, so much so that it rushed past us ankle deep, something struck my foot as we got to the doorway, it was a walking stick, I bent down and picked it up, while holding open the door for Marian to pass through, we were inside out of the storm, it was warm, dry and well lit. Marian was busy tidying herself up, her hair was wet; we were both wet and windswept. I said goodnight to her at their cabin door, she looked left and right and gave me a quick kiss on the cheek, as she closed the door with a wave.

Chapter Seven

I stood outside for a moment, and studied the heavy walking stick in my hand – I recognised it! It belonged to John Winthropp, with two P's, he needs this stick, for help with his gammy leg, what the hell was it doing on deck? He has trouble enough getting to the bar! I quickly went back to my cabin to check that he was there. I arrived back and pushed open the cabin door...

He was stretched out lying in the lower bunk...
"Are you awake?" I said, he didn't move, I put my hand on his shoulder and he sat up! Banging his head on my upper bunk! "Oh God! I'm Sorry!" I said, "I thought you were dead!"
"Why the hell should you think I was dead?" he said rubbing his head, and kicking his legs out into a sitting position, "Give me my flask out of my pocket" he asked pointing to his jacket, "I need a drink!"
I felt for his flask, and noticed his jacket was wet, "have you been out on deck?" I said handing him his drinking flask.
"What makes you ask?" he said, emptying his flask in one long gulp.
"Your jacket, it's soaked" I said.
"Not me, it's the steward" he said, borrowed it to go and look for my walking stick. I see you've found it – I left it in the restaurant, lunch time."

"Left it?" I said. "How did you get back here, to the cabin, without it?"

"The steward and his mate brought me back, a little too much bourbon!" he said. "Now, hand me my stick, I need the bog!"

I gave him his stick, and helped him up, and he went into the lavatory.

I started to change, getting my wet clothes off, John came out of the lavatory, tucking his shirt into his pants, just as the ship lurched and we both fell against the bunk beds, "that was a big one!" I said. "That sea is getting rougher by the minute!"

"The forecast is grim" said John, emptying the dregs from his flask by shaking it, determined to taste the last drop of alcohol as he held it high over his mouth. "What time is it?" he said.

"Gone midnight" I answered, looking at my watch. Then I shook my wrist, and listened, putting it to my ear, "bloody thing has stopped!" I said.

"Watches do not like seawater lad" said Winthropp. "Have you got any booze stashed away?"

"Don't drink" I said.

"Some bunk mate you turned out to be!" he said, and laid down back into his bunk.

I climbed up into mine, and put the light out…

Chapter Eight

Next morning, I was first up as usual, The Grey Ghost was still bouncing us around port to starboard, and then bow to stern. She was ploughing her way to Halifax Nova Scotia - And me? I was off to get my breakfast, I was hungry, plus there was a chance of my seeing Marian.

The restaurant was almost empty; the rough going was taking its toll. Food was the last thing they wanted to face, with all this bouncing around! I asked for my usual breakfast, eggs and bacon, with a mug of tea, and sat down, looking around to see any sign of Marian. I was sitting eating my breakfast when I saw Marian looking for me! I waved, and she came and sat opposite me. "Are you having breakfast?" I said.
"Just toast and coffee" she answered, looking around at the empty tables, "where is everybody?"
"I think they must be locked away in their cabins with a bucket and towel! This crossing is a rough one, there seems to be no let up."
"Did the stewards come to your cabin?" said Marian, "they woke us up early this morning."
"No, but I was up and out early, I was hungry" I said. "What did they want?"
"They were checking we were there..." she said. "There has been talk of missing people."

"How many people?" I said, "do you mean passengers?"
"Well I don't know who or what!" said Marian, "but they seemed concerned. You remember that blonde, Kate woman, she said her friend was missing yesterday?"
"That's right" I said, "she did say that, has anybody seen Kate to check if the other one turned up?"
"You know better than I" said Marian "they are your friends, not mine!"
"Don't be daft Marian, I don't know them from Adam, I only talked to them the once" I said.
"Twice!" said Marian.
"Okay, twice, but you were here with me the second time. I assure you, they are no friends of mine, and then I whispered, according to my cabin traveller, John Winthropp, with two P's... they, Elsie and Kate, are two ladies of the night, on the game! John said!"
"Well!" said Marian, "if that's true, I pity the two husbands they're about to join in New York. There are the two stewards I was telling you about... at the bar, with clipboards, he's seen us, and they are coming over. "Hello, any luck?" said Marian.
"We were talking to a passenger" I said, "Kate, only yesterday, she was on about her cabin mate who had gone missing. Have you spoken to her? Kate I mean?"

"What do you know of her?" said the steward "is she a friend of yours? A relation?"
"Crikey! No!" I said, "she just came over while we were having dinner and told us her friend was missing, gone to see a man and never came back! She said to us."
"Did she name this man? Or give a cabin number?" the steward asked them.
"No" I said, "nothing."
"What is your cabin number?" said the steward, "it's on my key – yes, cabin one three seven" I said, "I share with an American, John Winthropp."
"With two P's" said Marian, with a smile, there was a moments silence…

As the steward checked his list, "one three seven, yes, did you know you left your door open?" he said, "yes, of course, my cabin friend John was still in there, I came here for an early breakfast" I said.
"According to our list of passengers, you… You are James Bradshaw?" he said tapping his clipboard, "you are in that cabin alone! Not sharing! You were booked in by a shipping company."
"Yes, I'm going to join one of their ships in New York, I'm signed on as an able seaman, and, of course I am sharing a cabin!" I said in a loud voice.
"He was in the bottom bunk when I left this morning, fast asleep!"
"The only thing we saw in the bottom bunk was your kit-bag and a walking stick!" said the

steward, "no sign of anyone else, which doesn't surprise us, because it's listed as a single cabin, down to one James Bradshaw – and that is you!"

"That's ridiculous!" I said. "And that walking stick, that's his!"

"You were seen going into your cabin last night carrying that walking stick, it's been well described to us by a passenger" said the chief steward.

Marian said "Okay, I can explain that, he found it on deck last night."

"That's right" I said, "I rescued it from going over the side!"

"Did anything else go over the side?" said the steward.

"Such as?" I said stupidly.

"Such as the body of a woman, or should I say, two women? Mrs Elsie Castellani and Mrs Kate Sorbillo, who are now reported missing!"

"Have you checked their cabin? We only saw her yesterday? Sitting here, large as life!" I said, looking at Marian for back-up.

"We have checked their cabin, and there is no trace of them ever being there, no baggage, nothing. The towels are still clean, the soap is unused, and the two bunks have never been slept in. Nothing and nobody!" said the steward, "and now you tell me, you have an invisible friend – but he is not even registered by name as a passenger who boarded, <u>unlike</u> the two women."

"This is ridiculous" I said, "he was there in my cabin, I didn't make him up! Ah, and wait a minute! A steward talked to John, John told me a steward popped his head in and had a conversation with him, about the two women you are looking for, he said, the steward was convinced they were two prostitutes, on the game!"

"That bit is very true, unfortunately" said the chief steward, "now Ronnie here" pointing to his colleague, "is the steward in charge of this area of cabins… Did you pop your head into cabin one three seven, and chat to a John Winthropp, about two prostitutes?"

"*I did not*" said Ronnie, "that cabin is booked in the name of James Bradshaw, and nobody else, there is NO John Winthropp on my list who boarded!" he said.

"That settles that then" said the chief steward – and turned to talk to Marian "Did you meet this mysterious Mister Winthrop with two P's miss? The steward asked looking at Marian.

"No" she said, "I never saw him!"

"You have a guardian in your cabin Marian, I've never seen her!" I said.

"That's true…" she said.

"That will be – cabin two seven two, Mrs Maria Campanella, your guardian, you say?" said the steward, studying his clipboard.

"That is correct" said Marian, "she is escorting me to my family in New York."

"And you are Marian Rasero, is *that* correct?" said the steward.

"Yes I am" answered Marian, "that is correct."

"Thank you, we won't trouble you again Miss – Rasero!"

He then turned to face me, "but, I am afraid you sir, will have to answer further questions, regarding this invisible friend of yours."

"Just a moment!" I said, "yesterday he was writing a message he wanted to send from your radio room."

"You mean he took a written message up to the sparks?" said the steward.

"Yes, he said he was anxious to get it off as soon as possible" I said, "I saw it in his hand."

"Okay, follow me, and we'll go up to see the radio room and speak to the chief sparks" said the steward.

Chapter Nine

Marian said she would see me later, as she had to get back to the cabin. And the steward and I made our way up to the radio room on the top deck. I was introduced to the chief radio officer, [or sparks, as they are known], and I described John Winthropp to him... "No, no such person came in of that description, just some young Italian woman, she gave me a message to send, it's confidential though" he said.
The steward explained the situation and asked as a member of the officer crew, would it be okay if he checked the message? As the situation was so serious, people are **missing**!

After a discussion, he was handed a piece of paper and he studied it for some time, and then handed it back. "Okay" he said, looking at me, "you can go now, but we will talk later, after I have reported findings to the captain and the first officer."

I left the radio room, and made my way back to my cabin, to see for myself. There was no John Winthropp, the cabin was now locked, the steward must have a master key, or was John Winthropp inside? I got my key in the lock and opened the door, apart from *my* bunk, the place was pristine. No sign on Winthropp, the draws were empty, the cupboard was bare, no sign of him in the shower or at the wash basin. He truly had disappeared into thin air, nothing! But I *know* he was in this cabin with me.

Chapter Ten

It was now afternoon and The Grey Ghost bounced along through wave after wave, at full speed, by the sound of those engines at the stern of the ship, I walked, or should I say staggered there, to clear my head; one thing was nagging me, and I didn't want it to be so, that Italian woman handing in the message to be forwarded on to New York – could it be Marian's guardian? I've never see her, and what was the message? The steward had seen it, so he knew what was written and who it was sent to!

I left the stern of The Grey Ghost, she was throwing me about like a rag doll, it was no wonder there was so much sea sickness among the passengers, the bars and restaurants were half empty, mainly filled with seasoned passengers with sea legs! What a crossing <u>this</u> was!

I staggered back through the gangways and down into the passage to the restaurant. I decided I would have something to eat before I started feeling queasy... as I was ordering my meal I caught sight of Marian talking to the chief steward, I sat down at a table keeping my eyes on her, hoping to attract her attention.

A waiter arrived, placing a plate of food in front of me, it smelt good, then looking up again, in the direction of Marian, and she had gone. The chief steward was still there, but no Marian. He saw me, and waved a 'hello' and I waved back, but he turned away and left the restaurant. I sat and ate my lunch and gave myself indigestion, by eating it far too quickly. I returned to my empty cabin, and made a final search for evidence of John Winthropp, with two P's, ever being there... I could find nothing.

"There was a knock on my cabin door, it was the chief steward. "Just to bring you up to date" he said, looking down at me sitting on the lower bunk, "your lady friend, Marian, has given you a firm alibi, by saying she was with you all the time you were on deck, and yes, you did find the walking stick."
"Yes" I said, "I trod on it as I was leaving the upper deck, it was all awash with sea water..."
"Now" he said, sitting down on the bunk beside me, take a tip from a fellow shipmate my lad, and do not make any further contact with the young lady, Marian. Two passengers have definitely gone missing from aboard this ship, and a third person, the one you claim was in this cabin, cannot be identified as ever being aboard the Queen Mary, although" he said, "his name John Winthropp, with two P's, *is* listed as being on the passenger list, but, according to our records, he

never checked in! Now, of course you say he shared your cabin, so he too has disappeared."

"I told you, he was in this cabin" I said.

"Yes, but he never came aboard, to our knowledge, and was never allocated a cabin. This is a mystery yet to be solved" he said, standing up to leave.

"That piece of paper, in the radio room…" I said, "…you read it, what did it say?"

The chief steward looked behind him, and sat down again on the lower bunk next to me, "I have not told you this!" he said, pointing a finger at me, "it said Mrs A and Mrs B will <u>never</u> arrive at New York. They were <u>never</u> on board The Grey Ghost."

"Who sent it?" I said.

"It was" he said, "signed JW."

"John Winthropp" I said quietly, "that was his walking stick on deck, I told you he was on board! I told you…" I repeated. "Now, who was that message sent to? That could be the answer to this mystery." I said, "who was it?"

"I'm afraid that <u>is</u> confidential" said the chief steward, standing up once more to leave, "all I can say is, that two *very* influential New York Italian families, will not mourn the loss of two…" he hesitated, "shall I say, ladies of the night, G.I. brides, as members of their families, even if their two soldier sons do! Now!" he said, waving a finger at me, "just stay away from the lady Marian, and her guardian, you my lad are out of her class!"

Chapter Eleven

I went and climbed into my bunk that night, with my head spinning with thoughts and questions, all unanswered! Fortunately, next day, we were about to arrive in Halifax, Nova Scotia, so I went on deck to watch her dock and tie up along the quayside, it helped me take my mind off the mystery of the missing passengers. As I watched the many young wives gather to disembark to join their Canadian husbands, I watched as they paired off on the dockside, embracing each other with loving affection, however, there were one or two being met by someone who was obviously *not* their husband, I felt sorry for them.

The Queen Mary didn't stay long, which was a relief for the crew as Halifax was a dry town, no alcohol, no bars, "No nothing!" said the seaman leaning on the rail next to me, "next stop New York" he said, nudging me in the ribs, "now, there *is* a town!" he said. And that night, we set sail for America, and the ship I had signed on for…

To see the Statue of Liberty for the first time sends butterflies around your stomach, you really do feel a great sense of adventure, different sounds in your ears, and different smells in your nostrils. Everything is twice as big as anywhere else you have ever been. Even on board The Grey Ghost, as she docked between two other great liners, you could feel the excitement of the other passengers on board, rough seas and seasickness all forgotten...

This is America, nineteen forty six, I had my kit-bag on my shoulder once more, waiting to disembark, when I caught sight of Marian going ashore, with a tall dark haired figure, I couldn't make out if it was male or female, then Marian stopped, and saw me, she turned and blew me a kiss, I waved back as they both got into a waiting limousine, the biggest, longest car I have ever seen, and she was gone...

I spent the day in the offices of the Silver Shipping line, and got my papers and details of where the ship I was to join docked, and was told to sit down and wait, as there was a V.I.P. arriving. I sat in the reception of the splendid palatial offices for about an hour, studying my papers to pass the time, when suddenly the office came to life with people forming a line, from desk to desk, to the front entrance doors, a huge black limousine drew up at the doors, and a tall well-dressed man and two women came through the glass doors, to be greeted by the people inside with applause, as he approached the desk some six feet from where I was sitting, I recognised the face, of John Winthropp, with two P's, no sign of a limp, he was greeted in Italian and he replied with a handshake and in the Italian language, then he was taken through the doors behind the desk and was gone... without a glance! I jumped up and spoke to the desk clerk, "who was that?" I asked pointing to the closed doors.

"Our president, owner of The Silver Shipping line, who else?" said the desk clerk.

"Can you tell me HIS name" I said, "quickly?"

"Signore Antonio Rosero" he said, "why do you wish to know?"

"I knew his daughter, Marian Rosero" I said.

"I don't think so" laughed the desk clerk, "she's been at a finishing school in Europe, *not* in *your* class at all! Now go and join your ship." And he picked up a sheet of paper from his desk, and sarcastically read out in a loud deliberate voice, "The Silver Coin, Able Seaman, James Bradshaw. It sails tomorrow, goodbye!" he said, pointing to the exit doors.

James Bradshaw joined The Silver Coin at pier seventeen; he could see The Queen Mary across the bay, The Grey Ghost anchored between two glossy newly painted liners, with no sign of war service on *their* bulkheads... And James' eyes settled on the middle funnel of the gallant Queen, it was there he kissed Marian, now, just another passing ghost in the night.

The End

Gerhard Greenfingers

By Peter Maddocks

It all began when I was thirteen years of age, I was a lad born on a particularly dreadful bleak, damp, cold, half empty council estate at the wrong end of town, and my dad never existed apart from a letter my mum kept hidden away in a draw. She, like most of the women on the estate depended on benefits and cigarettes.

I for my sins, was a member of a gang called the wannabe's [we all wannabe rich] get it! We spent most of our daylight hours bunking off school and creating as much havoc and unpleasantness in the pathetic community as we could. For example, we would upset wheelie bins, break windows, smash garden gates [if anyone was lucky enough to have a garden!] Upsetting window boxes was a regular trick and chucking the contents at someone's clean washing, and of course if ever we got our hands on a spray can of paint we would decorate every doorway with some obscene message! All this for fun, or just for the hell of it, we had respect for nothing and no one.

It was school half-term as if this made any difference to us and the gang, we had been promised a school trip to the country, so we heard, so we thought, right – we'll have some of this, so, like well-behaved children we all put our names down for it. Sorted! We could get on this outing and show all the rest of the snotty bunch just what our gang is all about. The school teacher in charge of us, if I can remember was a Mr Zebador, or something like that, a black guy with a posh London accent.

It turns out that the reason for this trip was that it was a green culture outing, to show us city kid's part of the country away from the city, where flowers grow naturally and birds sing, regularly!

Not exactly on our gangs list of priorities, as you might imagine, we piled onto the bus and taunted various students that we thought warranted it!
Once at the location, we cut loose from the rest and ran into the wooded area, where we couldn't be seen; out of sight of those [who thought] they were in charge of us.

We ran through the trees and came across a large square area of young saplings. Fresh young trees, about two metres tall, all with labels on, just the job for a group of hooligans like us! We went through lines of them snapping each one in half, totally destroying the hope of them ever reaching maturity. I had reached the far side of the wood with young trees, having wrecked my fair share of them; my back was to the thickest part of the wood, very overgrown with large healthy trees reaching for the sky.

I had just snapped a particularly tall young sapling in half, raising my first in jubilation, when I was grabbed from behind by very large powerful hands and dragged physically through the rough undergrowth into the heart of the dark woods. When the dragging stopped I was face down in the dirt and something was wrapped around my ankles and I was hoisted high into the air, so much so, that I was spinning around like a top and could not see who or what, my assailant was.

Eventually I stopped spinning and threw up yesterday's meal… in front of me from my upside down position I could see a huge figure of a man covered in facial hair, he stood with a garden fork in his huge hands, for one terrifying moment I thought he was about to puncture me with it – fortunately he just turned the soil with it, beneath where I hung.

He spoke in an accent with a very deep voice. "You need be sick; you make me sick with your actions, all of you! Now, you see this hand?" he said, holding out an upturned open hand with his fingers spread.
"I see them" I cried in terror, thinking he was about to throttle me with his huge hand.
"What colour do you see on hand?" he said
"Colour?" I queried.
"Colour boy!" he shouted "what colour my fingers?"

They were green, "green!" I cried "green!"
"Good" he said, and he bent down and plunged his hand into the upturned soil beneath my upturned hanging body, "now boy" he said repeating his hand action in and out of the soil several times, "you hang there and watch!"
"Cut me down…" I shouted.
"You hang there and watch ground" he repeated, pointing to the earth, and then turned away out of sight taking the garden fork with him.

My hands were free, so I tried to fling myself up to grab the rope wrapped around my feet, but by now my strength had gone, the blood had rushed to my head, I had been physically sick, all I could do is just hang there accompanied only by the sounds of the woods. I could only stare at the patch of upturned soil beneath my head. But I looked again, the soil had vanished, now there was a ring of green shoots, growing green shoots moving up towards me fast, so fast, that within minutes my face was touching grass and leaves, then creeping plants were climbing about my hanging body, I was, I thought being eaten by the undergrowth. I was going to die, choked to death by plant life. I screamed and wriggled trying to free myself of this horror, when suddenly, the huge figure was back and cut the rope above my feet and I fell to the floor wrapped in green undergrowth. Face first with a thump!

"Now" said the voice standing over me, "how do you like being snapped in half, but you can be whole, trees broken in half are ruined. You are one very bad boy" he said.

I sat up, my head spinning, I tore at the vine like undergrowth that clung to my body and tried to stand up, only to fall down again! I was too weak. The huge bearded man said "Here boy, drink" holding out a tin mug. I didn't even ask what it was my mouth was dry with fear. I think it was cider, but it went down in one gulp.

"How did all that stuff grow so quick?" I said pointing to the scattered mess around me.

He said nothing at first, but held up his huge left hand, "what do you see?"

"Green fingers" I said, "I see green fingers" I repeated "so what?"

"Stupid boy" he said "go! go join your stupid friends."

I didn't want telling twice, I got up and staggered away from that place, out of the dark wood and into where I could see daylight. I went past the large patch of broken saplings and on towards the open space where the coach was parked. But it wasn't! There was no coach, there were no school children, and they had left! Gone without me, and surely that stupid teacher had had a headcount before leaving? Now what do I do? I'm miles from anywhere I'm stranded! I had no choice, I just had to return to the green finger man with my tail between my legs, I had no other choice!

I returned and told him of my plight. He said I could stay in his hut the night and he would put me on a bus in the morning. We sat and talked into the early hours mainly about trees, he knew everything about them, almost as if they were human, where they came from, what leaf they had, what fruit, everything! I eventually fell asleep and woke next morning to the sound of the woods. What a racket! I thought the city was noisy, I got up to the smell of bacon and eggs, Greenfingers was outside cooking on a cast iron fire, built like a fat tea pot, red hot with heat, and a two handled flap pan on top, full of sizzling bacon and eggs.

"Grab a plate and a fork and take some of this hot breakfast before it burns black" he said, "hurry boy!"
I quickly did as he said and helped myself, it was followed by a tin mug of tea, [I think it was tea] but I didn't care I was relaxed and well fed.
"I can put you on nine o'clock bus boy" he said, "we must walk to road soon and wait, I wave, he stop."
"You are not English" I said.
"Foreigner" he answered.
"What kind of foreigner?" I said.
"Prisoner of war foreigner" came the reply from behind me.

"Germany?" I said.

"Yes, Germany, I was young boy, like you. Conscripted" he said, pouring a second cup of whatever it was.

"What's conscripted?" I asked.

"No choice" he answered quickly. "Come on, you get bus."

We walked out of the wood past the broken trees, "can I come back and help you fix these trees" I said.

"You can come back" he said "you got money?"

"No I haven't" I said "we were on a school trip."

"I give you money" he said, reaching into his pocket, "if you want to come back, you catch same bus."

And yes, I did go back, it changed my life forever. Gerhard and I repaired all the broken saplings; he filled a wheelbarrow with soil for me to push and follow him up and down the rows between the broken trees. First Gerhard Greenfingers would plunge his left hand into the soil in my barrow, and then he wiggled his green fingers and quick as a flash, remove his hand and as I held the broken sapling upright the green fingers folded around the break with an iron grip. I had to count to ten out loud, and then he released the hand from the tree. And it was as good as new. Don't ask me how, but he repaired each tree the same way, left hand into the soil, a wiggle of the green fingers, out, and with a firm grip as I counted to ten it was repaired. It took us about four hours, but we repaired the lot. As we left for a pot of tea, I looked back at a field of upright saplings with their paper labels blowing in the wind, and as a result of that wonderful day, I myself have never looked back again.

I went to school and studied. I left my gang members calling me names, but I didn't care, I spent every weekend with Gerhard, learning about the trees, the hedgerows, and the countryside. I eventually made it into university; got a degree and here I am in government as a minister for countryside affairs.

And it was all thanks to my chance, all be it rough, meeting with Gerhard Greenfingers.

Yes we are still very much in touch; I had to contact him last week about a difficult situation. My job is as a go-between for town and country problems, a government official to liaise between police and public to calm things down, so to speak, not always easy. On this particular day, a message came through that a group of travellers had driven into a country village and taken up residence on a plot of land used as their [the villagers] cricket pitch. Totally illegal, however, the wheels on this subject in law turn very slowly. The village people were up in arms about the situation and the travellers were refusing to move on. The police could do nothing until papers were prepared and served, and as I said, this would take time… months even. I had to go and review the situation and calm everybody down. I first contacted my good friend Gerhard Greenfingers. Now he's not as young as he was, he would never tell me his age, but whatever it was, he still knew his countryside and his trees and hedgerows. I arranged to pick him up in my car and take him to this problem village. I had a brilliant idea, would it work?

Next day, I met with Gerhard, same place as when I was a lad, but now he had a proper home, a cottage with a splendid new thatched roof, whitewashed walls and lattice windows. I pulled his leg about it being a bit twee for a gruff, rough and ready foreigner like him! But he just shrugged and said something like beggars can't be choosers, as the local council had housed him there, because of his good work on the countryside.

I explained the situation to him and pointed out that tempers both sides were heated and it is up to us to either calm everybody down, or resolve the situation. I told him of my plan, and I can't be certain, but I'm sure I caught a smile on that rugged face of his. I reminded him of what he did to me on our first encounter!

We arrived at the village where we were greeted with locals carrying placards, and waving their fists at every official car that pulled up by the cricket green. We could see the problem immediately, cars with various caravans on tow had parked willy-nilly on their green. Large men and women were standing around shouting goodness knows what to each to each other, various children ignored everything and played or cycled over the villagers beloved cricket pitch…

Gerhard opened the boot of my car and took out a garden fork, probably the very same one I saw from my upside down position when I was a lad, then, without saying a word the huge frame of the man, despite his age he still looked menacing, moved off towards the cricket pitch ground…
I meanwhile, had to arrange a meeting of minds and get leaders from both parties together for a talk on how to resolve this situation, knowing full well that it would all be a waste of time and effort!

All would now depend on Gerhard, and his wonderful green fingers. While I kept both parties at bay, Gerhard and his garden fork went from caravan to caravan, first to disturb the ground with his fork as close as he could to each van, then each time, plunge his huge green fingers into each patch, wiggle them about, then move on until he had done the lot! I think the count was seven caravans. The local pub opened its doors and soon filled the bars; it was a fine day so people not involved in the meeting sat on benches outside and enjoyed whatever was in their glasses!

Through the open door of the pub I caught sight of Gerhard returning to my car, and after cleaning the soil off the prongs of his trusty fork put it back in the boot. I raised an upturned thumb at him and the hairy head nodded.

All we had to do now was wait. After about an hour or so, people from both sides came out of the pub, the villagers picked up their various placards and those who were travellers headed back to their caravans belching from lunch. Gerhard's green fingers had done the trick; each caravan was now so overgrown with every conceivable ivy and grass that each resembled a very green woven haystack!

The travellers had trouble finding the doors, some even had people inside [probably old folk!], banging on the walls unable to open their doors! Chaos! Disbelief! The only way to rid the vans from all the undergrowth was for them to get into their cars or vans and drive off the pitch wrenching them free from the grasses and plants, each making a ripping tearing sound as their vehicles wheels slid and strained to get a grip. The villagers looked on applauding each van as it ripped itself free and drove off! All seven eventually left a very messy cricket ground and after the car exhaust fumes had cleared- cheering villagers gathered on the cricket ground surveying the damage. Handshakes all round, from puzzled experts scratching their heads on how and where all this undergrowth had suddenly come from? But nobody cared, the travellers had gone, and the cricket ground, although worse for wear and tear, had been released from both traveller and the weird law of the land!

I made my way back to London after taking Gerhard back to his cottage, and after a cup of what he called tea, congratulating Gerhard on his fabulous green fingers. Fortunately on his left hand, because had they been on his right hand, a handshake farewell could have left me with all kinds of problems... perish the thought!

Weeks passed with a few minor problems that I had to cope with, and did until I had a call from an irate farmer on the east coast. The government, in its wisdom had agreed to a wind farm being built adjacent to his land and as a result was scaring the wits out of his cattle and as a dairy farmer he was losing out on his milk yield. I went and paid a visit to see for myself, it was a beautiful part of the coast flat and open, and of course, ideal for a wind farm, all above board, none were on his land, but they were very visible and they do tend to make a weird noise when there is a blow coming off the north sea. I could well see his problem!

As far as I could see, the farmers answer to the problem was either to move his cows to another field to graze, or somehow hide the wind farm and its mass of moving blades with a high fence of some sort – evidently the other field was out of the question because it was planted with barley. No, it had to some kind of fence to hide it...
"Trees... I thought" said the farmer, "but that will take years!"
"I might have the answer to that problem" I said, "leave it to me, meantime, I want you to plough a furrow the whole length of your field bordering the wind farm, just a couple of furrows wide, no more than that. I've got a phone call to make!"

I telephoned Gerhard, and he agreed to get a train and I would pick him up from the train station next day. Tomorrow, that is, in the morning about eleven o'clock.

I saw the farmer and his tractor ploughing the furrow as I requested that evening, the earth was turned over and it was moist and fresh.

Next morning as we arranged, I met Gerhard Greenfingers at the station. We stopped off at a cafe in the village for a cup of tea, a buttered tea cake and a chat. I explained the situation to

Gerhard and that I had taken the liberty of having tilled the soil along the boundary of the wind farm, had he any suggestions?

Gerhard took a ballpoint pen out of his pocket and started to draw on the paper tablecloth, "trees?"
"Yes" I said, "I thought trees, is it possible?"
"Poplar trees" said Gerhard, "close together, good tall trees."
"Excellent!" I said "so can you do it?"
"Has the farmer got horses?" he said.
"Well, I saw stables; I presume he's got horses. Why?"
"Manure, I need buckets of it!" Gerhard said.
"No problem" I said "you shall have it!"

The farmer did have horses; his wife ran a riding school for the local children, so manure was no problem. Gerhard, as usual wasted no time, he paced out the length of the field and checked the upturned soil, while me and the farmer's wife with the help of two lads and a girl from the riding school mucked out the stables, and filled several buckets with hot steaming horse manure.

Gerhard having finished his pacing up and down took off his jacket and rolled up the sleeve of his left arm. "Right I want manure buckets placed along this furrow" he said pointing, "about two metres apart, right up to the end."

This was eagerly done just as requested by the young helpers. "He's got green fingers" said the girl, "now what is he going to do?"
"Don't ask" I said "just watch."

Gerhard plunged his left hand with the green fingers into the steaming warm horse manure, the girl screamed YUK! And all three jumped up and down holding their heads in amazement! Then Gerhard quickly plunged his hand from the bucket deep into the upturned soil. This he did quickly one after the other along the row until he reached the second bucket of manure. Then he plunged the green fingered hand into that bucket of manure and repeated the process all along the furrowed line, until he reached the last bucket, where the farmer's wife stood with a fresh bucket of water and a towel. p.s. don't try this at home!

"What on earth was that all about?" said the young girl holding her nose.
"He must stink something awful" said the two lads together!
"He knows what he's doing rest assured" I said, "wait and see!"

The farmer turned out his cows into the field having milked the herd. "The situation is getting worse" he said, "I'm well down on my milk today. I hope that big hairy friend of yours knows what he's doing, I'm getting desperate!"

"You will have to wait and see" I said.
The farmer's wife came over, having emptied the bucket of water that Gerhard had used to wash his hand and arm… "I'll get your friend a nice glass of cider" she said, "the big feller has earned it!"

That evening Gerhard and I booked rooms for the night down at the local pub. Next morning we had a hearty breakfast before setting off to Hilltop Farm, when we arrived there was great jubilation on the farm.

We were greeted by the farmer's wife shouting at the top of her voice… "It's unbelievable! Look! We have trees! Hundreds of them, twenty… No thirty foot high, hiding all those dreadful wind farm turbines…"
"That will please your cows then" I joked.
"It's unbelievable" she said; wait until I tell the girls at my pottery class!"
"The less talked about this the better" I said, "please be happy at what has been achieved and leave it at that."
"Don't be silly" she said "waving to her farmer husband, "there's a journalist coming for an interview at one o'clock."
"Now listen" I said "the department I work for does not like publicity, and Gerhard hates being interviewed."
"Well it's too late now; here comes the photographer from the local paper. Hi there…"

she said waving. "Here we are you've got the right farm."

My first thought was I had to get Gerhard away from here, "where's Gerhard?" I asked.
"Talking to my husband, admiring the fact that we haven't got a view anymore" she said still waving.

I caught Gerhard's eye and signalled for us to leave, and walked back to the car. Gerhard arrived and got into the car and I immediately drove off before the cameraman had a chance to aim his lens at us!
"Everything ok?" asked Gerhard.
"Yes of course" I lied. "I just thought we should get going now it's a long drive back."
"We should catch train back" said Gerhard.
"I've got to drive back" I said, "this is a company car. Just sit back and relax, you did a great job back at Hilltop Farm."
"Good trees, Poplar" he said I always like making trees…"

It was a three hour drive back to the city. So I suggested we get a meal and I would book Gerhard into a hotel, and I will pick him up and take him home in the morning. The drive back went well and Gerhard had a doze and managed not to snore too loud, I swear I could get a whiff of horse manure now and again. I managed to park the car and we made our way to a restaurant I know and use quite often, it's a friendly Italian place with a pleasant cosy atmosphere and good food. We sat and ordered our meal and a glass of wine for me and a large pint of beer for Gerhard. The usual television was on up at the bar and unfortunately we were sat facing it. Just as the soup arrived and I reached for the bread in a basket, the television screen showed the fine figure of the farmer's wife of Hilltop Farm being interviewed about what she called the magic windscreen of Hilltop Farm!

"Yesterday" she said waving her arm in the direction of the now tall Poplar trees, "yesterday all you could see over there were ghastly wind turbines, then we had a visit from a magical man called Greenfingers, and that is just what he had – green fingers!" Then she went on giving every detail, the buckets, the manure, a full description of Gerhard and his action, the report finished with twenty four hours later and the camera slowly panning along showing the long line of tall swaying Poplar trees…

Gerhard stood up spilling his soup and upsetting his chair "she talks about me on television" he said, pointing at the screen.

"Something wrong with the soup?" said the waiter picking up Gerhard's chair.

"No" I said. "I'm afraid it's your television."

Gerhard took a very large swig of his beer and slamming down the glass on the table he stormed out of the restaurant. I managed to calm my friendly waiter about my colleague and told him I would be back for my meal later, and then I rushed out to catch up with a very irate Gerhard.

"Sorry about this" I said, I tried to tell them to keep quiet and be grateful for what we had done for them."

"Make fool of me" he said "you promised me it was all big secret."

"Village gossip I'm afraid" I said.

"Last time…" Gerhard said poking me in the chest, "no more, finished!"

"It will probably blow over" I said, "it's only a small village, not exactly big news. Come back and finish your meal, then after a good night's sleep you will see it as just a load of county gossip in the morning."

Next morning Gerhard was still in a bit of a mood, but I was sure he would calm down once he was back in his thatched cottage. As we entered the village leading to Gerhard's cottage there seemed to be an awful lot of traffic jamming up the village square, my heart sank when I saw television equipment being unloaded from a large van… the media are here for Gerhard, I also recognised a few journalists from previous encounters I've had with the press.

I had to keep going and get through the village, if they were to see Gerhard it would be a free for all. The story of Hilltop Farm must have gone national!

I got us through the village okay, then I made my way a further mile or two on and stopped at a roadside cafe used by lorry drivers. Gerhard by now was not happy and I had difficulty coaxing him out of the car and into the cafe. "I'll get you a hot strong coffee as long as you promise not to move or speak to anyone while I make a phone call" I said. I got a reluctant grunt and a half nod of the head. I used the phone box in the café and phoned headquarters to put them in the picture, however, they were well aware of the situation having read the newspapers and seen television. I was to get Gerhard Greenfingers back to London, the forestry commission and the European agriculture people wish to interview him in private. On no account let him loose on the press or television.

I put the phone down and re-joined Gerhard and after ordering myself a large coffee, I came up with a brilliant idea... I went around the café tables asking which truck driver was heading for London. One young driver told me he was just about to leave, I thought he was Dutch by his accent, but I was wrong, he was German. Perfect! I explained Gerhard's predicament to him, and that we were ordered back to London by government officials. So he agreed to smuggle us both aboard his truck and give us a lift to London. I left my car keys with the café owner and told him it would be picked up in a day or two, and I left him a hefty tip!

I told Gerhard of my plan and he was anything but happy about the situation. But when the young lorry driver cut in speaking German to him, he calmed down and we all got into this huge truck. We kept our heads down going through the village, so as not to be seen, and we were soon gliding smoothly along the motorway heading for London. I myself hardly said a word as Gerhard and the young driver were too busy talking German to each other. After a journey that seemed like days instead of hours, we arrived in the city of Westminster, London, and following a fond farewell and gratitude to our young truck driver friend, I managed to get Gerhard to head office without mishap!

Once there we were interviewed and shuffled from office to office and department to department, all asking the same questions. Eventually a top official from the forestry commission claimed Gerhard for himself. He personally was going to give him a safe haven, and as Gerhard Greenfingers favourite interest was in the health and safety of trees, he was going to join the commission doing just that! And as he now trusted me, I would be in charge of his welfare, making sure he was housed and fed properly, but most of all keeping him well away from the media.

We spent the next two years traveling around looking after countryside and hedgerows, and of course thanks to Gerhard's green fingers… planting trees; hundreds, no thousands of fresh new trees created by Gerhard's special magic formula, the commission were encouraging the planting of more birch, elm and oak as they were getting scarce, after those two years Gerhard requested retirement, he was now in his eighties, and moved back to where he was born, Germany, in the south where the brothers Grimm were also born, the home of fairy tales…

Sadly one day I had a phone call to say that Gerhard Greenfingers had died, and he had requested that I personally would scatter his ashes, in the wood where I first met him as a boy and had vandalised his sapling trees.

This place he wrote, although a foreign country to him, had helped him discover that he who loves trees, loves more than just himself – I could not agree more…

The End

The Housesitters
By Peter Maddocks

Chapter One

Jane and Paul Zucchi received a letter from their solicitor in England; they live in a three bedroomed villa in Coín, a town in Spain, having retired there three years previously. The letter stated that owing to a death in the family of a distant relative in America they have been named in the will. 'Please come to a reading of said will on Friday the fourth of July at my offices in Chancery Lane, London.'

I don't have relatives in America" said Paul.
"No, but you know I do!" said Jane taking the letter to the window to read again, "on my father's side, the Italian family that came from Naples and settled in America, New Jersey I think, father never furthered it though, you know how conservative he was."
"Had an Italian surname though" said Paul putting the kettle on. "*Bonelli* – can't get more Italian that that!"
"Very much so" said Jane, "I'm proud to have been a Bonelli girl, but dad liked to think himself very much an English gentleman."
"That's because he worked in the city" said Paul. "He wore a black jacket and striped trousers if I recall."
"You leave him alone; he gave us all a good upbringing, private school and everything" she

said, "now back to this will reading, and pass the chocolate biscuits please!"

"Well" said Paul, "we must go and hear what they have to say. I'll book us a flight on line, when does it say the reading is?"

"American Independence day, July the fourth" said Jane, "couldn't be more appropriate."

"Very patriotic" answered Paul from the computer, "shall we make a week of it?"

"No, ten days" said Jane, "I want to do some shopping, go to the theatre…"

"Okay" said Paul "ten days it is! Now what about leaving this place? Ten days – empty villa, could be risky, don't forget those <u>books</u> you look after in that safe!"

"Well when Dino and Kelly went away for their anniversary holiday, they booked Housesitters" said Jane from the kitchen.

"Phone them and ask if they still have the sitters number" said Paul, "and I'll check the local English language freebie papers."

Chapter Two

That evening Jane made contact with the couple who had the Housesitters, but learned they'd returned to England for good months ago.

"No matter" said Paul, "I've found a couple here in the paper, and they are local, they are English, no British I think. It's a Scottish name by the look of it. I'll give them a call."

"Also" said Jane, "Kelly said her husband Dino is having treatment for his diabetes evidently he has poor circulation in his legs and has difficulty walking. Arteriosclerosis, she says."

"Sounds painful enough trying to pronounce it" said Paul laughing.

"No laughing matter" said Jane, "it can lead to strokes or a heart attack."

"Shame" said Paul, "sorry, thing is, they are the only Italian couple we know here in Spain."

"Well we are a bit isolated here on the outskirts of Coín, I mentioned that when we bought it" Jane said, "but you were so taken with the property, we don't even have close neighbours. At least Dino and Kelly are related to me, vaguely, and they are *American* Italian remember!"

"All the more reason for us to take on Housesitters" said Paul writing down a phone number out of the local on-line paper, "but you <u>are</u> happy here aren't you Jane?"

"As long as you are happy dear, I'm happy" she said. "Now give this housesitting couple a ring and let's take a look at them!"

Paul made the phone call and arranged to meet with the couple at Bar Rosa in Alhaurín el Grande, the next town to Coín. Evidently they had just arrived back from Cadiz, where they had been housesitting a property for a family in Scotland.
"They sounded quite young" said Paul, "he had a Scottish accent."
"Did you speak to both of them then?" asked Jane.
"Well, she answered the phone, and then put me on to him."
"Her husband?" said Jane mopping the kitchen floor.
"Now how do I know?" said Paul. "These days it could be anything."
"Be as well to know" said Jane moving the water bucket. "After all we will be turning our property over to strangers for ten days or so."

Chapter Three

Next morning Paul and Jane drove to Alhaurín and parked the car on a side road. They found Bar Rosa, a café facing a roundabout with a stone cross in the centre, as instructed on the phone the day before, it was a warm sunny morning so they sat at a table outside with comfortable cane chairs and ordered coffee.
"How do we recognise this couple?" said Jane looking around the empty seats.
"He has long dark hair and a beard and she is blonde, so he said."
"And he was right" said Jane "because here they come now, crossing the road."

Paul stood up and put his arm in the air. The young man with the beard waved back as they both dodged the traffic to cross.
Paul introduced himself and his wife Jane.
"I'm Logan" said the young man with the Scottish accent, "and this is my wife Jenny, short for Jennifer" he joked.
Jane smiled a smile of relief about their relationship, "are you also from Scotland?" Jane said to Jenny.
"No" she said, "I am originally from Poland, but I have lived in Scotland for six years, until we came to Spain three years ago."
"Same as us" said Jane.

Paul ordered more coffee and after some small talk, got down to business. Logan said back in Britain he was really a computer engineer and his wife Jenny a trained nurse. But they had got fed up with work and the rotten weather, and they decided to seek adventure in Spain. They hadn't the money to buy a property so they became Housesitters, and so far have always been successful in finding a roof over their heads.

"How do you cope between properties?" Paul questioned.

"We have a very comfortable camper van" said Logan. "It's no hardship living in it for a week or so, and of course it's still our form of transport."

"A bit smelly at times" interrupted Jenny, "and short on storage, but we cope!"

"The clue is to keep everything minimal" said Logan, "don't collect clutter!"

The conversation got to cost and how many other properties have they stayed in and have they got references and recommendations? All seemed in order, and the interview went well. Jenny and Jane had lots of woman talk and seemed to like each other. Logan was a bit 'hippy' for Pauls taste, but seemed likeable and intelligent.

An agreement was made and a date was set for the couple to take over. They would leave their property to fly to England on the morning of July the third, so if they, the Housesitters, would move in on the afternoon of that date and remain until a phone call for the date of their return. They have been told to only book one way, as there could be a delay in the reading of the will.

The day arrived, Paul and Jane left to get the plane from Malaga airport to fly to Gatwick having left the fresh set of house keys in a secret place for the Housesitters to collect and move in.

Logan and Jenny did just that on the afternoon of the third of July and moved into the property.

Meanwhile in Hoboken, New Jersey, in the USA, a man called Antonio Mancuso is anxiously on the telephone to London, arranging the delivery of four landscape paintings to an address in Coín, southern Spain. They had arrived at London Heathrow airport and were to be collected and transferred onto a flight from Gatwick to Spain. This was to be handled from a solicitor's office in Chancery Lane, London and to whom he was now talking… "I want you to get your *best man* to handle this transaction…" he said, "he is to travel with these four paintings and see that they arrive safely at the address in Coín in Spain. Expense is no object; a cheque will be paid as soon as they acknowledge that my people have received the paintings… Yes, of course they are for an exhibition… Yes, to be displayed in a gallery in Malaga. Now, are my instructions clear? Good, we will be in touch.   By the way" he continued, "that *best man* that you will be sending to accompany my goods – his name is Pietro Grasso, *is that clear!* Okay, goodbye."

Chapter Four

Now back in the villa on the outskirts of Coín, Spain. The Housesitters Logan and Jenny are surveying the contents of the house. Jenny is searching through the bedrooms while Logan checks everything on the ground floor...
"How are you doing up stairs?" shouts Logan from the foot of the stairs.
Jenny comes to the door of the master bedroom and then onto the landing, "not a sign of any jewellery" she said, "there's got to be a safe somewhere."
"Your right" said Logan, "I'll keep looking, no luck so far, but there seems to be one hell of a lot of paperwork in this small study. There is lots of up to date computer equipment though, plus Skype and other communicative gear. He is a man that is in touch with the USA. There is a huge map on his wall with flags and stickers on various states."
"Have you phoned for the van yet?" shouted Jenny.
"No, got plenty of time for the fucking van" shouted Logan. "So let's reckie the place first shall we."
"You know my feelings when it comes to clearing a house, get in, get loaded and get out!" shouted Jenny.
"The van will deliver us boxes mañana!" shouted Logan, "now find something of value for fuck sake!"

The phone rings and Logan answers… "Hello!"
A woman asks "are you the Housesitters?"
"Yes, I'm Logan" he said. "Who is this?"
"My name is Kelly, Mrs Kelly Tarullo, wife of Dino Tarullo, who is a colleague and associate of Paul and Jane Zucchi, I'm just making contact so that if there is anything you can't manage, or you need help, don't hesitate to contact me, my number is…"
"I've got your number here on the pad in front of me Mrs err…" stammered Logan.
"Mrs Tarullo" she answered, "Mrs Kelly Tarullo…"
"Okay Mrs Kelly" Logan interrupted, "should I need to call, I will get in touch, whereabouts are you? … Yes lady, I know you are in your house, but where *is* your house? In Coín? Whereabouts exactly are you in Coín?" He makes a note on a notepad in front of him, "okay, thank you… Yes, I will keep in touch, thank you, and goodbye!" He puts down the phone.
"Who the hell was that?" said Jenny coming down the stairs.
"A fucking nosey neighbour" cursed Logan, "you're right about clearing this house quick, we're being watched!"
"How do you mean *watched*?" said Jenny looking out of a window.
"No, not out there, in Coín, at this address" he said waving a note book, "I'll get on to the van people and tell them to step on it, get this place cleared –

and fuck off!" he said. "There has got to be a safe hidden somewhere!"

"Try the garage" said Jenny.

"Not really" said Logan, "it's <u>always</u> in the house."

"Let's eat and open a bottle" said Jenny, "I'm starved."

"Yes, and I'm dying for a drink, lets crack open one of their bottles of wine, you rustle up some grub, then get your knickers off and we can try out their bed! But tomorrow is for real; we can't hang about in this place." Said Logan

"Spagboll Okay?" she shouted from the kitchen.

"Might as well" said Logan, "there's a lot of *Italian* names floating about in this Spanish house, fuck knows why!"

Chapter Five

At the solicitors' office in Chancery Lane, London, A Mr James Conway solicitor meets with Pietro Grasso, who has arrived to take possession of the four paintings from Heathrow.

"All the paperwork is in order" said the solicitor James Conway, "and a plane ticket is booked for you, here are the details, and this is all the paperwork you will need to land your paintings at Malaga airport. You leave at 11:45 tomorrow morning, so it's up to you to collect from Heathrow and book them into Gatwick this afternoon. Is that clear?"
"Okay, it is clear and understood" said Pietro Grasso, I leave the van at Gatwick airport, and post you the car park ticket in this stamped addressed envelope with the van keys – correct?"
"Correct" said James Conway, "and good luck."
"What could be easier" said Grasso, "piece of cake!"
"As you say - piece of cake" answered James Conway seeing him out of the door. Then the solicitor goes back to his desk and picks up the phone to call his secretary in the next office. "What time am I seeing Jane and Paul Zucchi tomorrow?"
"Eleven o'clock" she told him.
"Fine, make sure all their papers are on my desk. I've got to call New Jersey as soon as I've dealt

with them, and this person Antonio Mancuso is not a man to be woken up in the middle of the night to discuss travel arrangements!"

Chapter Six

Next morning in the villa in Coín, Logan and Jenny wake up both with hangovers witnessed by three empty wine bottles on the floor by the bed.
"Christ!" swore Logan, "what time is it?"
Jenny struggles to find a clock, "half eleven" she said.
"Fuck!" shouts Logan, "what time is that fucking van supposed to be here?"
"Don't ask me" said Jenny cleaning her teeth in the bathroom "you booked it!"
"I think it was twelve thirty" Logan said looking out the bedroom window, "well at least it hasn't arrived, thank God – last thing we want is that twit Colin banging and yelling at the door!"
"Too right!" said Jenny pulling on a dress, "the less notice we attract the better."
"Notice?" said Logan "you mean attention, you silly bitch!"
"Okay, <u>clever</u> let's hear you say it in Polish!" she yelled.
"Fuck off!" he answered.

The van arrived at one fifteen with the driver Colin and a butch girl called Beverly.
"What the hell are you doing bringing *her*?" said Logan at the door, "we are shifting furniture – or have you forgotten you bone head!"

"She's okay" said Colin, "strong as a fucking ox she is, I've got scars on my body to prove it, she's got a grip like iron!"
"I don't want to hear about your sex life, there's work to be done! Get her to use some of that brute force on that leather settee over there…" he said pointing.
"It's a big 'un" said Colin, "it'll take three of us to shift that!"

The three tackle the settee pulling and pushing it to the open door then tipping it on its side to push and pull it through – "Hey!" shouted Jenny, "Look what was under that settee."
"I can't see anything" said Colin looking at the bottom of the piece of furniture…
"Not there" shouted Jenny, "there, on the fucking floor! It's a safe!"
"So that's where they keep it! Under the fucking settee" said Logan, "crafty bastards!"
The group forget the settee and stand around the safe buried in the tiled floor, staring at it.
"Now what?" said Colin.
"Now we get it open" said Logan.
"You've got keys?" said Colin.
"Course I haven't got keys, you dimwit – I've got to force it open, you get on loading that furniture while I attend to this" he said.

While Logan hacked at the safe in the floor with a heavy mallet and chisel, Colin and the two women continue to try to get the huge leather settee out through the front door, Colin calls to Logan, "how long have we got to clear this place?"

"At least ten days" shouts Logan still hacking at the safe in the floor, "why?"

"It's going to take at least a week to get this brute through this door" said Colin

"Use your fucking brains! Get a rope around it and get the van to pull it out."

"What if it tears the leather" said Colin

"Then you lose out trying to sell it, you bonehead!" said Logan. "Hey! I've bust the fucking lock! I've got the safe open!"

Colin rushes in, leaving the women pushing the settee, "what's in it?" he shouts, "money? jewels?"

"Books" says Logan, "books, four bloody rotten books!"

"Who puts books in a safe?" said Colin.

"Accounting books" said Logan, flipping through the pages, "some kind of accounts, all in American dollars, thousands of 'em!"

"Great!" cries Colin, "the money must be in this house!"

"Not this much money" said Logan. "Somebody is shifting lots of money around, lots and lots of money, all the details, dates, goods, sales, customers addresses, banking details, all here in this one" he said waving it under Colin's nose. "It's all in this little black book dated sales of 2012"

Chapter Seven

Meanwhile at Malaga Airport Pietro Grasso has had to wait for his four pictures to turn up, all his papers were in order, eventually they arrive, each packaged in a wooden crate and numbered. He has a van and two men ready to load parked outside the airport terminal. They are loaded and Pietro Grasso and the two men head for Coín forty to forty five minutes away. He phones Dino Tarullo but his wife Kelly answers, explaining that Dino is ill, but she was expecting the call and everything was arranged and in order. No problems she had said.

Back at the Zucchi house the settee had been dragged out and was now in the van. Jenny has cleared the wardrobes of clothes and bagged them up in black plastic bags, other various trinkets were boxed and she was about to tackle the kitchen, while the mighty Beverly and Colin were loading computer equipment and a huge television onto the van. Logan having studied the accounting books decides to put them also into the van.
The telephone rings – Logan signals for Jenny to answer it and everyone else to stay quiet. It was Jane Zucchi phoning from London.
"Hello" said Jenny in a bright chirpy voice. "Yes all is fine, no, there have been no phone calls, and everything is good. You have nothing to worry

about; your house is in safe hands. Logan is now in the kitchen cooking lunch, he's waving to me to say 'hello' to you. Hope all goes well in London, bye bye, thank you." The group all make the thumbs up sign as Jenny puts down the phone.

Pietro Grasso arrives at the Dino Tarullo house, and they unload the four boxed paintings, and Pietro pays off the two van men and they drive off to return to Malaga airport. Kelly Tarullo has made lunch and apologises for the fact that Dino was not well enough to greet him. But she hopes he will be well enough to talk for an hour to two this evening, however, she has made all arrangements for acquiring a safe house to store the four pictures and for him to live in, while sales were completed. A vehicle for him has been purchased and is in the garage with all the necessary documents. The small town house has been purchased legally and has been made safe; it is in the old town of Alhaurín el Grande, in the centre. It only has a front entrance with a steel door, no back exit, and the roof terrace has been sealed off. She gives Pietro the keys to the house and car and they sit out on the terrace for lunch.

During lunch they discuss the merchandise, four valuable pictures disguised as landscape and seascape scenes, two Picasso's, one Gauguin, and an Andy Warhol screen print, total value anything from two hundred million American dollars.

Pietro asks if there is someone to help him move into the house with the pictures, Kelly said she has a guy coming this afternoon who lives in Alhaurín, and he was safe, Dino knows the family and he has used him many times for deliveries and collections. Pietro told her customers are already lined up for the pictures, the Picasso's go to Russia and Gauguin to the Middle East, and the screen print, Gibraltor. As soon as the money is banked they will be collected and he can get back to the states.

"I've been told to return with a copy of the 2012 account books" he said, "are they here?"

"No" said Kelly, "I will have to go to the Zucchi house, I have keys to the safe and house, we can go after lunch, it's only twenty minutes away…"

"No" he said, "I'm not leaving the paintings, the account books can wait, the sooner I can get this valuable merchandise locked safely away the better!" Kelly agrees saying she will pick up the account books and deliver them to him at the safe house in Alhaurín.

Chapter Eight

Next day, day three in the Zucchi house Logan and Kelly wake up with another hangover from the Paul and Jane Zucchi wine cellar, Logan tries his luck with Kelly lying naked next to him but she's having none of it, and leaps out of bed and into the bathroom.

"Plenty of time for love making after we've cleared this house and are on our way to a market" she shouts cleaning her teeth, "get that prat Colin and his Amazonian girlfriend up and let's get cracking!"

"Okay, okay" said Logan, "you get some coffee on the boil, and I'll sort the others out."

It was now almost midday when a car pulled into the drive, Colin rushes in shouting, "we've got fucking visitors!"

Logan runs to a window to see an elderly woman getting out of a car and studying a half loaded van in the drive. "It must be that nosey fucking neighbour that phoned!" said Logan.

"Now what do we do" said Colin, "she's seen us and coming in!"

As Kelly Tarullo gets to the door and views the mess – "What the hell is going on here!" she screams, dialling a number on her mobile phone.

"Get that phone!" shouts Logan.

And big Beverly grabs the elderly lady shaking her like a rag doll as the mobile phone skids along the floor and into the hole of the battered safe.
"Where's the books that were in that safe!?" she screams still being almost crushed in the huge arms of Colin's girlfriend Beverly.
"So they *are* important then?" said Logan.
"You don't know what you've got yourselves mixed up with" said Kelly struggling to get free, "they'll cut your balls off for this mess!"
"That's not nice" said Colin.
"They? Who are they?" asked Logan. "Will they be prepared to *pay* for those books?"
"It's you lot who will pay" she said, "with your fucking lives!"
"That's not a nice thing for an old lady to say" mocked Logan.
"Shocking language!" shouted Colin laughing.
Jenny grabbed Logan's arm "let's lock her in the lavatory and get the fuck out of here" she said.
"I don't like the sound of this, chuck her in the downstairs lavvy and lock the door" said Colin to Beverly who was still holding Kelly in a firm arm lock.

Beverly drags Kelly into the downstairs loo and shoves her in shouting "I can't lock the fucking door the key is on the inside!"
"Use your head" he answered, "and shove a chair under the handle, "she's an old lady, and she ain't going nowhere.

Beverly does this and is joined by Colin shouting "old ladies always need the lavvy so you're in the right place!"

Chapter Nine

Not this old lady, inside the loo she removed the lid off the cistern and lifts a plastic bag out of the water containing a fully loaded .38 magnum revolver. She takes the revolver out of the plastic bag and calls out… "Are you there? Please, I'm a little claustrophobic, be a darling and let an old lady out, I'll behave, I promise, I *know* where the *money* is hidden…" she said in a pleading voice.
Colin shouts "Logan! She knows where the fucking money is hidden!"
"Okay" he answers "get her back here!"

Colin kicks away the chair and pushes open the toilet door, Kelly is sitting on the loo pointing the .38 and as she gets sight of Colin she lets off two shots throwing him back and killing him instantly. As Colin hits the ground Beverly watches in horror and takes a bullet in the head, falling dead over the bleeding Colin. Once out Kelly moves into the lounge to confront Logan, but he and Jenny hearing gunshots make for the back entrance to escape outside and into a vehicle. Kelly by now has two shots left; she shoots at the fuel tank and misses as their camper van containing Logan and Jenny smashes through the gates at the end of the drive… the van containing furniture and the accounting books is still parked outside the garage doors…

Kelly returns inside the house and dials her sick husband telling him of the goings on in the Zucchi house, he tells her to sit tight and he will make phone calls and phone back. Ten minutes pass as Kelly watches out of the window. The phone rings, her husband tells her two men are on their way to clean up the mess. And has she recovered the accounts books? Kelly tells him they are in the truck outside, had checked that they were safe before phoning.

"Don't scare Pietro Grasso at the safe house" said her husband, "he may panic and we've got valuable merchandise to shift, collect the books, and when the 'cleaners' arrive get back here with them, on no account phone London. The less anyone knows about this *happening* the better. Leave the gun for the 'cleaners' and get out of there – Now!"

Kelly collects the accounts books and puts them in the boot of her car, then picks up the gun and wipes it clean of prints and chucks it on the floor next to the two dead bodies, then she gets in her car and as she drives through the smashed gates another vehicle arrives and flashes it's headlights as Kelly drives out and past the black BMW with two men, she ignores them as she passes and makes her way back to her own house.

Chapter Ten

Meanwhile at the small townhouse in Alhaurín el Grande known as the safe house, Pietro Grasso an American Italian with a taste for Spanish cuisine, is busy cooking when his phone rings, he answers it having wiped his hands on a tea towel. A voice says this is an international call from somewhere in Russia asking if their merchandise is available for collection. Pietro gives a code name and number identifying which two pictures are to be collected and continues to make arrangements. He then contacts the Dino Tarullo house and informs the sick Dino of the details. Tomorrow afternoon at 3 o'clock during siesta – A quiet time, a black Renault van will arrive, two men, one Russian, one Romanian will collect two disguised paintings. Money will have been deposited in the bank, details that you gave to the Russian.
He said "you will have been informed of the total amount."
"Okay" answered Dino, "I'll check with the bank in the morning if the money is in the account – fine – I won't phone, if it isn't I'll call and get reinforcements to you, to sort the Russian and the Romanian out! Is that clear?"
"Okay" said Pietro, no call money paid, if you call, no paintings handed over. We sort them out!"
Pietro puts down the phone and dumps his overcooked Spanish meal in the bin and phones for a takeaway!

Kelly Tarullo arrives back at her house and collects the account books out of the boot of her car and takes them into the kitchen, puts the kettle on and goes to a cupboard and takes out a bottle of Jack Daniels and pours herself a large one.

"I'm back Dino!" she shouts from the bottom of the stairs "do you want coffee or bourbon?"

There was no answer; she finishes her drink and takes the account books into the study and puts them on the desk. She then goes up to the bedroom to check on Dino her sick husband.

He is sitting up in bed with his eyes closed; Kelly touches his shoulder and his eyes open, his lips move but there is no sound.

"I can't hear you?" she says, he again tries to talk, but again there is no sound, Kelly goes back down stairs and gets pen and paper, back in the bedroom she hands Dino a pen, with difficulty he takes it from her and scrawls... *'I think I have had a stroke – can't talk, can't move'* –

Kelly phones for an ambulance, Dino continues to scrawl a note, *'take the four accounts books to the safe house'* she puts down the phone saying "three books Dino, there are three books!" Dino shakes his head and writes *'4 books, three big books one small black book, dated 2012.'*

"No black book Dino – just 3 big books." Dino writes <u>Black book most important, has codes, phone numbers, picture details and delivery dates, plus bank information</u> to receive payment!' Kelly shouts "for the last time Dino – there is <u>NO black book!</u>" and before she could finish, Dino slumps forward, he is now in some kind of a coma.

The ambulance arrives and Dino is taken with Kelly to the local hospital in Malaga for urgent treatment. After examination the doctors confirm that it is a stroke and the word neuropathy is mentioned signifying nerve damage, which can cause loss of feeling in hands and feet coupled with extreme weakness and other unusual symptoms, and that the next twenty four hours are crucial – Kelly must stay with him at the hospital.

Chapter Eleven

Next day at the safe house Pietro is aware that having received no telephone call, all is well to proceed with the collection of the two hidden Picasso paintings that afternoon at 3 o'clock, when a black Renault van will arrive. And arrive it did on time outside the safe house metal front door in the very narrow street in the old town of Alhaurín el Grande, there were two occupants in the van, both dressed in black, wearing dark glasses and jockey caps. The smaller blonde one is at the wheel and the one receiving the two paintings from Pietro has a dark beard and long dark hair, little dialogue is exchanged and the two boxed Picasso paintings disguised as landscapes are loaded quickly into the van, then after a brief handshake is driven off out of the old town of Alhaurín el Grande.

As they head into Malaga <u>Logan</u> the <u>Housesitter</u> says to his driver <u>Jenny</u>, "it went like a dream – now this is the delivery address according to this little *Black Book!* First I phone <u>our</u> bank to confirm the Russians have paid in the cash, and then we make the exchange and get the fuck out of this country and start to live the <u>GOOD</u> <u>LIFE</u>…"

The widow Kelly Tarullo, Paul and Jane Zucchi, left Spain for good a month later, Kelly returned to Hoboken, New Jersey, having delivered the remaining two paintings to the clients and thereby with only half the money! She entered a retirement home [so they say], Paul and Jane returned to England having been left a full size portrait of her late father Franco Bonelli in the will, but no money. Pietro Grasso mysteriously disappeared and was never seen or heard of again!

The End

The Lakes

By Peter Maddocks

Chapter One

Harry Keepax was a man who had worked all his life to make a success of his business, and then the computer came along, a magical machine that would change all our lives, and that it did! Harry supplied animation materials, paint, cell, paper, everything including the camera and equipment he rented out to the small cottage industries of talented people producing animated films for television. The computer changed it all and threw most of it out of the window and on to the garbage heap.

Okay he wasn't short of money, he was always a careful man and he also knew how to make what money he had work for him! But here he was, a fifty-two year old a man who had looked after himself lived for his business to a degree that it cost him his marriage, his ex-wife had taken off with a young animator from Argentina two years ago and a costly divorce ensued.

He had a nice mock-tudor detached house in Purley, south London. It was beautifully and tastefully furnished by the attractive wife with a taste also for younger men. Not that Harry was plain, he wasn't he had looks and a good physique, but what he had in looks he lacked in personality. He was a work horse, a money machine; as far as his wife was concerned he was bloody boring!

So the wife had gone, now so had his business, what now? He didn't have friends; he had acquaintances, business people, all casual, the occasional drink type people. His sex life was almost non-existent, just a one night stand following a glass or two too many. Nothing to write home to your mother about, that's if you still had a mother. No, something or someone had to change, he decided he would change his country; he would pack up, let the house and move to Spain!

His mother was Spanish so he was lucky enough to be bilingual, he could speak it like a native, or so he thought until he stepped off the plane at Malaga airport, the language he heard the locals speak wasn't the language his mother had taught him, she was educated, she was a teacher with three or was it four languages. However, he knew enough to get by until his ears were tuned in to the local dialect. He had moved inland away from the usual tourist spots. A mixture of nationalities had mixed in pretty well everywhere you went in Andalucía but to have the Spanish language, local or not, was a bonus.

Harry rented a villa in the mountains of Mijas, a white village high up overlooking Fuengirola and the Mediterranean, the views from his rented villa were magnificent; he didn't jump in and buy property unlike most the Brits, he wanted to look around first, he was a careful man, he wanted to make sure that this is what he wanted before committing to permanent ground.

After about three mouths of eating out, walking the bars and the shops, life became tedious, even with the sky being blue and the sun being hot day after day. His conversations with the people he met were getting repetitive. The weather, sex, or lack of it and the world news at large saw Harry looking at his finger nails bored out of his skull.

It's time to look further afield he thought, a couple he had met last weekend were going on about the lakes up past Pizarra. How peaceful and beautiful they were and if you gave the weekend a miss, as Spanish flock there for picnics by the water, and instead choose a weekday you could have the lakes to yourself.

Chapter Two

Harry decided to try them out today, Tuesday, always a boring dull day as far as he was concerned, even some of the Spanish bars and cafés closed on at Tuesday. So he fuelled up his car, and of course it was fine sunny day, Harry set off for the lakes having written down information on how to get there!

The journey was very pleasant, the mountains got larger and greyer as you passed field after field of trees full of fruit with fields ploughed fresh for melon and strawberry, then surprisingly he came upon a wind farm at the beginning of the approach to the lakes, winding roads, purple grey mountains turning black and spilling its dusty debris across the tar-mac, and after turning off the main highway pine trees huddled together like Londoners in a subway train. Then he saw them, the lakes, majestic silver and blue green waters as far as the eye could see. It was as the couple had said, well worth the journey.

Harry parked his car in front of a large café restaurant facing a lake that lay in a crater, as if some kind of volcanic eruption had purposely hollowed out a great bowl and filled it with water, Harry looked over a waist high wall and looked down through the trees at the water's edge. On his right there was a gap in the wall and stone steps went down to the water with two or three steps submerged, ideal for swimmers to take off with ease. Fish could be seen, large and small in groups and occasionally disturbing the water's surface with the flick of a tail.

Harry crossed the road and sat at a table outside the café ordering a coffee with a wave of the hand to a man in an apron behind the bar. It was a very pleasant place he thought, quiet and peaceful, little sign of tourist visitors as yet as the season hadn't started. The coffee arrived and a half hour of uninterrupted calm was enjoyed by Harry Keepax.

He had just ordered a second cup of coffee when through the gap in the wall opposite, he was aware of a very attractive woman rising up the steps from the lake, she came straight over the road towards him…

She stood by his table and smiled, "sorry" she said in English, "but you remind me of someone I used to know."
Harry being a gentleman stood upright, "someone pleasant I hope" he said.
"Very" she answered, "may I sit down?"
"But of course" said Harry arranging a chair, "coffee? tea? Or a cold drink perhaps?"
"Coffee would be fine" she said stroking the rear of her skirt as she sat down.

She was very beautiful thought Harry, tall elegant with shoulder length red-brown hair; he couldn't see her eyes as she wore large dark, almost black sunglasses. She looked cultured and sounded educated. No sound of an accent, pure, clear, cultured English!

"You must think me very forward coming over to you like this" she said as her coffee arrived.

"I assure you" said Harry "the pleasure is all mine" then offering his hand said, "My name is Harry, Harry Keepax."

"Hello Harry" she answered taking his hand. "I am Isabel."

"Lovely" said Harry, "Isabel or Isabella?"

"Just Isabel" she said.

"Are you a resident or a tourist?" asked Harry stirring his fresh coffee.

"Oh I've been here forever" she said with a wave of the hand.

"Really!" said Harry, "well I have just arrived!"

"In Spain?" said Isabel.

"No, no, I mean here at the lakes, I've been in Spain around three months."

"A veteran!" she mocked.

"No, I know Spain well" Harry answered, "I speak the language fluently, as a matter of fact, my mother was Spanish."

She sipped her coffee without answering…

"Do you speak Spanish?" said Harry.

"Yes I do" she answered, "but I prefer to speak English."

"Are you English?" said Harry.
"I have an English passport" she said and looked about, as if she was now bored, and Harry immediately recognised this look from his ex-wife, and quickly changed the subject.
"Are you with someone?" he said.
"No" she said, "I'm with you!"
Harry laughed and said "and very pleasant it is too!"
"That's better" she said, "your face lights up when you laugh. Are you married?"
"Not any more, I'm an Ex." He said.
"So am I" she said, "ex everything – however I must go, thank you for the coffee."
"Hold on…" said Harry, "just let me pay and I'll walk with you" he turned and paid at the bar, she, Isabel was standing by the chair she had been sitting in, then as he turned to join her, she had gone! Vanished!

Chapter Three

Harry stepped down to the table, looking left and then right, nothing, not a sign of her. He quickly crossed the road to the gap in the wall again, nothing, just empty steps down to the water's edge, although the water was disturbed at the bottom somewhat.

Harry looked around him, then returned to the bar at the café, "una cerveza por favor" he said to the barman.
"One beer" said the barman in perfect English! "Have you lost that lovely lady?"
"She just got up and vanished" Harry said, "did you see her go?"
"No Señor, I saw nothing" he said, "but she was very beautiful" he added.

Harry drank his beer, and then went for a walk by himself; he walked around looking at the scenery for an hour or so, and then made his way back to his car. As he approached the café restaurant opposite where his car was parked, sitting alone at the same table was the lovely Isabel.

Harry stopped and said, with arms outstretched "you just vanished into thin air! I searched for you!"

"I'm so sorry" said Isabel, "that's why I'm waiting here, hoping to see you again. It was very bad manners, I do apologise."
"No need" said Harry, "you are here now. I wanted to ask you to lunch – or dinner?"
"Lunch would be lovely" she said. "Okay if we have it here?"
"Why not" said Harry, "I've done with walking for today."

They both found a suitable table in the restaurant with the best view of the lake, the barman acted as waiter as it was off season, made quite obvious by the lack of people, you could count them on one hand and that included Isabel and Harry! They quickly scanned the menu and ordered lunch; Isabel had mixed fish and Harry had grilled hake, a bottle of dry white wine arrived with two glasses...
"Cheers!" said Isabel raising her glass.
"Cheers!" said Harry, "thank you for your company."
"It is I who approached you if I recall" Isabel said.
"That's right" said Harry, "you said I reminded you of someone."
"The father of my son" she said as she downed her wine in one.
"Husband...?"
"No" interrupted Isabel, holding out her glass for more wine, "my step-father."

There was a long silence, "he, your step-father fathered your son!?" said Harry leaning forward.

"My mother was an alcoholic" she said, "so he used me instead – as often as he could."

"And you let him?" said Harry leaning back in his chair as the fish arrived.

"Had no choice" she said, "no lock on my bedroom door, nowhere else to go; for my sins, I began to enjoy it, that is, until I found I was pregnant. Then I panicked and so did he, the bastard. They blamed a boy I knew who lived nearby. He paid him money to claim it was his." She poured another glass of wine.

"And where is your son now?" said Harry picking at the fish on his plate.

"Dead" she said, "three days after his birth."

"I'm so sorry" Harry said putting his hand on her arm.

"So am I" she answered. "I can never have another, he is buried out there somewhere…" with a wave of her hand, "they never told me where."

"Are these so called parents still around?" said Harry with his hand still on her arm.

She quickly pulled her arm away saying "both dead, thank God. Can I please have some more wine."

Harry filled her glass and as the empty plates were taken away he said, "and you say I reminded you of this creep of a man?" he said, wiping his mouth with a napkin.

"Everything but the eyes" said Isabel, placing a finger on Harry's forehead, "you have beautiful warm brown eyes, his were cold and blue like steel."

"And the boy who claimed to be the father in his place?" questioned Harry, draining his wine glass.

"Oh he just took the money" she said. "And parents, both his and mine came to an agreement, but as the child died, they were *all* off the hook!"

"Listen…" said Harry, taking out a pen from his jacket pocket, "this is my telephone number, I'll write it large on this clean napkin, please phone me, I want to see you again, I'm now a single man, I don't have any bad habits apart from being boring, that is! I wash regularly and I still have all my own teeth! Ring me, please."

Isabel said nothing, but did pick up the napkin and suggested Harry order coffee and brandy. Harry put up his hand to attract the barman and asked him for two coffees and one brandy, and then to Isabel he said "I have to drive back to Mijas."

"Are you going to run away from me already?" she said, "I was going to show you a secret place, it's not far," the brandy and coffee arrived. "My *very* secret place" Isabel added.

"Then I will get the bill and you will take me there, I love secrets!" said Harry calling over to the barman who he paid and tipped, and who had also noticed the numbers on the napkin! "That's mine" said Isabel picking it up.

"Sorry about that" said Harry "couldn't find a piece of paper to write on."

"No problem" said the barman, "enjoy your day."

"Do we walk? Or drive?" asked Harry as they left the restaurant.

"We drive, it's a bit of a steep climb, and I'm a little drunk" she said, "is this your car?" she got into the passenger seat, and as Harry climbed in behind the wheel she kissed him on the cheek.

Chapter Four

She directed him up through the narrow roads and tuned towards the sky, until they could go no further. Two massive pine trees grew almost on the edge of the world with a wide clump of soft grass between them, and then a panoramic view of the Spanish countryside lay what could be a mile beneath them, and with blue grey mountains either side.

"Quite breath-taking" said Harry, "a beautiful secret place, you could almost fly off this edge, if we were two eagles we could glide for miles…"
"I wish I was an eagle" said Isabel as she sat down on the grass.
"You are a beautiful woman" said Harry looking down at her, "far far more beautiful than an eagle."
"Make love to me" she said pulling him down to her by his hand.
"Out here? In the open!" said Harry looking about him.
"The eagles won't mind" she said as she pulled him over her body.

Harry kissed her full lips and his passion possessed him, pushing her clothes aside he ran his hands over her body, she loosened his shirt and trousers and wrapped her fingers around his penis… and suddenly the animal in him took over as they locked together in passion, she clawed at his back digging in her nails as he thrust into her open legs, time and time again… there was a slight breeze that rustled the trees above them and was topped by the screech of an eagle as it passed overhead.

"He's seen us" said Harry, and they both laughed, as each adjusted their clothes; they kissed again, and then turned to lie on their backs in the warm sun.

"Now it's your secret place" said Isabel.
"Correction" said Harry turning to kiss her again, "<u>our</u> secret place."

They returned to the restaurant for coffee, this time as a couple, "can I take you home before I go?" said Harry.
"I am home" she said, "just a short walk away. You get back to Mijas."
"You'll phone me" said Harry, where's that napkin?"
"In my skirt pocket" said.
"Show it to me" he said, "I want to make sure you have it." She took it out of her crumpled skirt pocket and put it on the table. "Good" said Harry, "now when can I see you again?"
"I'll ring you" she said, "isn't that why you gave me your number?"

"Of course" he said and he kissed her, "see that you do."
"I will, I will" she repeated, "now go!"

He kissed her again, then having paid for the coffees he waved goodbye from his car door and drove off. She waited for a moment, ordered a brandy from the barman, "on the house" he said as he delivered a full glass of Spanish brandy, she raised the glass as a thank you and downed it in two gulps, stood up and straightened her twisted skirt and left – leaving an empty brandy glass and a napkin with a telephone number written on it in ink…

Chapter Five

Harry Keepax was walking around the narrow streets of Mijas, the white village high in the mountainside overlooking Fuengirola and the Mediterranean. It was Tuesday a whole week since he left Isabel by the lakes, she hadn't phoned; he had written both his land line number and his mobile on that napkin in the restaurant. He decided that he must drive up to the lakes again and find her. He climbed the very long line of stone steps up to the road where his car was parked. Drove back to the villa to check his answer phone, and if it was still blank, drive up to the lakes.

As he turned into his drive it was blocked by a police car, two officers were standing nearby and a third was at the villa trying the doors. As he got out of his car the two officers approached him...
"Are you Señor..." he looked at a paper in his hand, "Keepax? Harry Keepax?" he repeated.
"Yes I am Harry Keepax, what's wrong?"
"We are here to ask you questions about a young woman" he said.
"What young woman?" answered Harry.
"We are not sure of her name" he said, "only Isabel."
"Yes, Isabel, I do know an Isabel, she lives somewhere by the lakes, is she hurt?" said Harry anxiously.

"A young woman was pulled from the lakes this morning, pronounced dead from downing. Do you know this woman well?" said the first police officer.

"O my God! Are you sure it's Isabel?" said Harry.

"We are not sure of anything other than this woman was last seen in your company last week by the barman at the restaurant. It is he who gave us these telephone numbers" he said holding up the napkin.

Harry looked closely at the napkin, "yes I wrote those numbers last week, last Tuesday, I left it with Isabel…"

The policeman interrupted by saying, "you must come with us back to the lakes for further questioning and you must identify the body, if it is who you say it is, Isabel, you said – yes?"

"I hope to God it isn't her" said Harry. "Yes of course I will come. Shall I follow you in my car?"

"No, leave yours here, you will travel with us" said the police officer as they all got into the police car.

When they arrived at the station near the lakes the police officer in charge was called aside by a senior officer, while Harry was taken into an interview room. The police officer returned and threw down a folder onto the table.

"Have you an address for this woman you call Isabel" he said.

"No" said Harry, "I only met her once, it was mostly in that main restaurant by the lakes."

"Well" said the officer, "it's embarrassing, he opened the folder, here is a report on the finding of a young woman's body, a young <u>dead</u> woman's body in the lake. It was put into a room here," he gestured with his hand, "for identification, and it has vanished!"

"How do you mean, vanished?" said Harry standing up from the chair.

"She has gone! It was there this morning, now it isn't. Like I say, embarrassing" said the police officer. "It was in there waiting for the coroner! So, you are free to go, and with my apologies. We of course will take you back to Mijas."

"Not yet you won't!" said Harry. "I'm going to find Isabel first, and make sure she is safe! Then I will return, and we can go on from there.

Chapter Six

Harry left the building and headed for the restaurant by the lake by taxi. On arrival he first asked to see the barman and ask not only if he had seen Isabel, but how he got that napkin with his phone numbers. The barman, he was told will be back to work around four thirty. It was only three o'clock, so Harry ordered a beer and sat at a table to gather his thoughts... he could get a taxi to take him up to the secret place, or he could try making enquires at bars and coffee places around the lakes.

Half an hour passed and a waiter said "are you Señor Harry?"
"Yes I am" he answered.
"Up in the restaurant there is a young woman asking for you to join her" he said.
Harry made the stairs up to the restaurant in three great strides, it was empty but for a figure at the window table at the far end waving – it was Isabel. Harry rushed through the empty tables and picked her bodily up off the chair with a mighty hug.
"Thank God. It *is* you!" he said, "I've just been put through hell."
"Put me down Harry" she said, and then shouting to the waiter staring at them from the far side of the room... "Two coffees, two brandies!" and she sat down looking at Harry, who was staring at her as he too sank down into a chair.

"I thought it was you" he said putting his hand to his head, "a poor woman has drowned in the lake, this morning well they think she has," he stammered, "they, the police, that is, have lost the bloody body!"

"Stranger things have happened around these lakes" said Isabel, "but as you can see" looking down at herself, "it wasn't me!"

"Thank God" said Harry as the coffee and brandy arrived, and he raised the glass and downed it in one gulp! He turned again to the waiter beckoning for a refill.

"You've had a bad day" said Isabel sipping her brandy.

"However it can now only get better!" said Harry as the waiter refilled his brandy glass.

They sat talking for half an hour or so when Isabel said "let's go for a swim!"

"What now?" said Harry.

"It is the best way to make a fresh start after the day you've had" she said "We can get a bottle of wine, a couple of glasses, and get a taxi down close to the lakeside where I know a perfect private place for us to swim…"

"I have no swimming gear" he said.

"Oh yes you have" smiled Isabel, "the perfect swimming gear – your skin!"

"Skinny dipping!" said Harry, "at *my* age!"

"At any age" said Isabel, "I never do anything else, and costumes are for tourists! Come on, you get the wine and I'll get the taxi, and get him to pull the cork she shouted!"

The taxi ride was short and as Harry paid the driver Isabel started off down through the pine trees, clutching a bottle of wine in one hand and two plastic glasses in another. Harry followed, it was steep and it was hot, the afternoon sun had heated the sandy earth beneath their feet. At the bottom it was just as Isabel had promised, a small horseshoe shaped cove, perfectly private, with a warm sandy beach on the edge of the lake. Isabel was already down to a bra and panties when an out of breath Harry arrived.
"Come on, get those clothes off!" said Isabel pulling the cork from the bottle.
Harry removed his shirt and his socks and shoes.
"Trousers!" shouted Isabel, "I've only felt you naked, and I haven't <u>seen</u> you naked yet."
"All in good time" said Harry stripping down to his underpants, "where's my wine?"
"Coming up kind sir" she said in a mocking voice.
"This is lovely" said Harry, "what a great idea, and you – you look wonderful."
"Then come and kiss me" she said standing legs apart and arms spread wide – Harry obliged with a long passionate hugging kiss that made her breathless. They both sank into the sand and sipped their wine.
"You really do remind me of my step-father" she said stroking his naked chest.

"I'm not surprised" said Harry, "the *creep* was always half naked taking advantage of an innocent sixteen or was it fifteen year old girl?"

"I was fifteen and he wasn't a creep, he was a beautiful man, it was my drunken mother who was the creep. I made him love me, I would take a bath or shower and leaving the door open, through which he would watch me in silence from outside. And I would stand up and expose myself to him." She said pouring out more wine, "until he couldn't help himself but come into the bathroom and close the door. I had never seen a man's penis, so I locked the door and unzipped his flies. It was beautiful and erect; he stood up against the door breathing heavily while I played with him. I loved it! I was in charge of this man; I had taken him off that drunken bitch of a useless mother."

Harry drunk his wine in silence, he didn't say a word, she reached into his underpants and Harry dropped his wine and rolled over on top of her.

"I want to see yours" she shouted! "Let me play with <u>your</u> penis!"

"What happened to these so called parents of yours?" asked Harry.

"Oh they died" she said, "that silly cow of a mother was always smoking in bed, and one night they were both drunk and everything went up in flames."

"And where were you?" said Harry.

"Oh I ran outside and waited for the fire engine. Do you realise how quickly a house can go up in flames?" she said. "Now, no more questions take those silly pants off and make love to me – then we can swim."

Harry realised Isabel, the woman he was with in the restaurant was now talking like a fifteen year old girl, "let's swim first" he said, and stood upright.
"Okay, if you must" she said, and jumped up and clung on to him like a limpet, arms around his neck and her long legs wrapped around his waist, "walk us into the water" she said, in the woman's voice… "Come on, walk us both in!" she repeated.

Harry put his arms around her holding her naked body close and splashed into the lake, his feet left the edge of the sand and they both fell forward into the water still clinging to each other, first Isabel was totally submerged with Harry striking out with his two arms to swim on top, but still Isabel clung to him, dragging him under, then rolling like a log so that she was now on the surface and he was underneath. This action continued three or four times as they glided twisting into deep water, then they were gone. Both submerged, silence and yet more silence – then nothing…. nothing but a ripple or a splash as a fish surfaced the water.

Both Harry Keepax and the woman Isabel had vanished beneath the deep cold waters of the lake…

Chapter Seven

That evening the police started making enquires as to the whereabouts of Harry Keepax, he had said he would return to the station with any news of this Isabel woman he knew, and they would then return him to Mijas. They had phoned his villa, and there had been no reply, so he hadn't returned home. A taxi driver reported taking a couple to the lakeside and both had been in the restaurant drinking. Nothing was found and the search was called off.

Next morning a fisherman reported a body in the water, it was male about fifty or fifty five years of age. It was Harry Keepax, the police officer who had interviewed him, now was needed to do the identification, "I want a guard on this body, we don't want to find it missing later on when the coroner arrives" he said.

The fisherman who found the body was interviewed, and turned out to be the very same fisherman who found a young fifteen or sixteen year old girl's body in almost the same place – *four years ago!*

"Her name was Isabel" he said…

The End

The Magician
Peter Maddocks

Chapter One

When I was struggling to make a small business work to keep the wolves from my door, I produced posters by hand or silk screen advertising, showing what was on at the local cinema or who could change the world of politics or even a simple bring and buy sale at the local church.

One day a man turned up at my little cramped studio door saying he was doing a turn [not a gig], at the town hall and wanted two hundred posters advertising his arrival, his act was as a hypnotist! He went under the name of Captain Henry Morgan, a pirate, who could steal your mind and control your actions for the price of a ticket. He was a big man, six foot something; around forty five, with strange starring dark eyes, black long hair and a moustache, and he also spoke in an accent that I couldn't identify through a well-trimmed black beard. You could practically smell the sea on this bulk of a man made pirate.

We agreed a price and a date for delivery and he handed me two free tickets to see his act, and to his credit also paid me a deposit! I worked out a poster rough which he approved and I got to work and cut the stencils by hand and produced two hundred posters, solid black lettering on a yellow paper background big bold lettering you could read in seconds as you passed by in your car, bike or top of a bus. Captain Henry Morgan was pleased with the result and paid his bill in full.

The day of the show arrived and I and a very full town hall theatre audience arrived to be either entertained or frightened out of our wits.

Henry spotted me taking my seat from the stage and waved me to come up and watch from the wings. "You'll be safe from my powers there, no point in making a fool out of a working colleague" he said.

He was amazing, he had the audience in the palm of his hand, first he told them all to put their hands on the top of their heads, and not to take them off until he told them to. This, the audience did, well most of them that weren't terrified! He then clapped his huge hands together and told them – in a loud strong deliberate voice…
"Those of you that <u>can,</u> remove your hands from your head when I shout remove …" he then followed by a loud shout of "remove!"

A smattering of the people in the audience released their hands but the majority struggled to unlock their clasped fingers or remove them from their heads, those that could, said so and laughed and applauded those that couldn't, looking ridiculous as they struggled to do so.

Captain Henry Morgan then invited six people to come up on stage so that he could free their hands, leaving half the audience trying desperately to remove theirs without success.

Once on stage, the six were told each to perform a silly act once he gave command for their release
"One two three all six remove!" he shouted, and each performed a silly act that had the audience in stitches, one barked like a dog, another walked about the stage flapping his arms like a chicken. Everyone thought it was hilarious; Henry then clapped his huge hands together and shouted…
"Remove hands!" And they all removed their hands from their heads in the audience with ease. He was fantastic!

Chapter Two

Ten years or so have passed since I saw that show with Captain Henry Morgan.

It was a wet Friday night in a village pub just south of the city of London, that a poster caught my eye with a photograph of a dark bearded man advertising himself as Lazlo Varga Magician Extraordinaire.

I swear this man was the Captain Henry Morgan, the hypnotist of some ten years earlier! Or was it someone very much like him? I ordered my drink at the bar to accompany my pub meal and I asked the barmaid, a woman of mature years, with hair dyed blonde and far too young a fashion cut surrounding a face of stone...
"Have you seen this magician called Lazlo Varga?" I asked.
"I've seen him" she said, "he scares me to death, he undress me with those black staring eyes."

The thought almost put me off my meal as she poured me a glass of red wine.
"He reminds me of a hypnotist I once knew" I said, "but that wasn't his name."
"He lives around these parts" she said, "he sometimes pops in for a pint and a look at my cleavage. The man scares me – something very unhealthy about him!" And she gave a shudder

that shook off one of her dangling earrings. I left her looking for it under the bar as I returned to my meal table.

Chapter Three

It was the next day that I caught sight of him in the village; it was Captain Morgan as I knew him. You couldn't mistake him, a big six feet plus square man with long black hair and a beard now streaked with grey, he was picking up fruit from the counter of a shop with his huge hands. Yes, it was him! Now with a different name and a different occupation, a magician no less! He looked in my direction, but gave no sign of recognising me, no real reason why he should; all I did was produce and deliver his posters.

Today I am a free-lance journalist and a writer of fiction, I've had a few books published, one that almost made it as a film, I was paid an advance but have heard nothing since, and that was some six months ago, but I live in hope!

This Lazlo Varga man was interesting, the fact that I knew him in another life and another profession gave me an idea for a book, and I wanted to meet him again and get to know him. Now I must revisit the pub and get details of his next act from that poster displayed in the bar.

Chapter Four

The following day I decided to visit the pub and have a lunch and make notes from that poster, so I could investigate further the escapades of Captain Henry Morgan now posing as Lazlo Varga, Magician and Entertainer!

It was while I was taking down the time and place of the show that I was aware of young slim man standing by me, looking over my shoulder reading my notebook, I stopped writing and faced him…
"Sorry" he said, "didn't mean to pry; only I'm the magicians assistant in that show."
"Fantastic!" I said and introduced myself, "I have met this Lazlo before, but not as a magician."
The young man's face stopped smiling "what? When was that?" he said.
"He was a hypnotist then" the smile suddenly returned.
"Oh I see" he said almost relieved. "Yes, he is a man of many talents, are you coming to see the show?"
"Yes I am" I said, "I'm a free-lance journalist; I could probably do a revue on it."
"Splendid" said the young man, "Lazlo always welcomes publicity, especially if it's free, I'll give you a ticket, and I've got some in my bag. Care for a drink?" he added.
"Thanks" I said, "I'll have a glass of red wine."

The drinks arrived via the ageing barmaid who I now discovered was the wife of the owner of the pub, well almost ex-wife, as they evidently live separate lives.

All this information was coming from the young magician's assistant who is on his third or fourth glass of red wine, ideal for a loose tongue and a journalist's pen. He [the assistant] was thirty five, and has worked with Lazlo for five years, before that he was a medical student at Exeter University, but became disenchanted not only with medicine but also university life and the lack of money in his pocket!

"Oh so showbiz is well paid then?" I said taking notes.
"<u>NO</u>" he said laughing and waving his empty glass at the barmaid for a refill. "Its pocket money, but I enjoy it."
"How do you pay your rent?" I asked, looking at him as he downed yet another glass of wine.
"I work with Lazlo he's a…" he hesitated… "He's the church warden," then belching "Ooops! Pardon me" he said banging his chest with his fist, "and I'm his assistant at the crem – crematorium, stoker I think it's called!" he laughed.
"You <u>both</u> work in the crematorium?" I furthered the question with added interest.
"Yes" he giggled. "We both make bodies disappear!" then he added quickly, sitting upright

as if to steady him-self, "in the ovens and on the stage! A disappearing act!" he belched again… "I think I should go to the loo" he added getting up and staggered off to the gents knocking over a glass and a chair as he went.

Chapter Five

The barmaid came over and tidied up by wiping down the table… "Did you find your earring the other night?" I asked. She stopped and looked me up and down, "sorry" I said, "only you dropped an earring at the bar."
"Oooh yes!" she remembered "damned thing is always coming off" and then changing the subject quickly she pointed to the loo and said "do you know that young man?"
"No" I said, "I've only just met him."
"Watch him! He's dodgy" she said, "as a coot! If you know what I mean…" she added.
"No, I'm just interviewing him, he's the magicians assistant" I said.
"That's what they <u>all</u> say" she said as she wiped down the table top once more. "I just don't trust his kind."
"He's had a drink too many" I said and then I suddenly saw Lazlo, nee Captain Henry Morgan, walk into the pub.
"Look out!" said the barmaid, "here's the <u>other</u> one!" And went behind the bar putting on an artificial smile across her granite face, "can I help you sir?" she said in her best polite voice.
"You can" said the big man, "have you seen my so called assistant?"
"He's in the loo, throwing up our best red wine" she said wiping the counter with a soggy cloth.

"Oh God" he said. "Give me a pint of your best ale. Bloody fool, we've got a show to do tonight."
"You'll need all of your magic to get him ready" she said plonking a pint of ale down onto the counter.
"Put it on my bar bill" he said.
"Plus half a dozen glasses of red wine and that broken glass I'm about to pick up!" she answered pointing.
The big man downed half his beer in one gulp and wiped his black beard with his sleeve.

I stood up and held out my hand, "can I introduce myself" I said, "I'm a journalist just making notes on your activities" I said.
"<u>What</u> <u>activities</u>!" he said leaning forward and refusing my hand.
"Your showbiz activities" I said. "Your assistant was telling me all about it."
"I see" he said, downing the rest of his ale, and wagging the glass at the barmaid for a refill. "I hope he wasn't running off at the mouth."
"Oh I think he gave me enough information for me to give you a revue" I said.
"In that case, you had better come and see me work" he said, "that's if I can get this silly sod sober enough in time" said the magician pointing to a pale faced assistant coming out of the loo.
"Christ!" he said, "I think I ate something that didn't agree with me."

"The trouble is…" said the magician, "you didn't eat anything. Are you fit enough for work? We've got a *special*, just arrived, and then we've got a show tonight."

"I'm okay" he said, "I'll stick to coffee, don't worry."

"Come on then" said the magician, then turning to me he said "have you got tickets for tonight?"

"Yes I have, your assistant gave me two" I said.

"Was that before or after he *ate* too much!" said the magician.

I ignored that remark saying "what time are you on stage?"

"Eight o'clock" said the magician, "don't be late!"

"Did I hear you say that you now have work to do at the crematorium?" I said stupidly.

"That is our business and none of yours!" said Lazlo Varga, "did this idiot go on about our work there?"

"No" I said "he at first said you were the church warden."

"That I am" he said, "now leave it at that. Enjoy our show!" And with that they left the pub.

"Weird couple those two" said the barmaid, "you owe me for two red wines" she added, holding out her hand for the money.

I paid for the two wines the assistant was supposed to have paid for, and asked the barmaid what she knew of the church and crematorium.

"Why should I know anything about a crematorium" she said. "Are you trying to be funny?"

"No" I said, "I'm sorry but evidently those two work there disposing of bodies."

"What!" she cried, "I thought they were showbiz not monkey biz! I'm going to wash my hands – we know the manager of that place, he's a pal of my ex, they play golf together."

"What's his name?" I said getting my note pad out.

"John" she said, "John Bellfield, nice guy – a bit thick!"

"I'll have a word with the manager of the crematorium" I said, "if only to confirm that those two work there – there could be a story in this!"

"Do you play golf?" said the barmaid pulling a pint.

"No I don't" I said.

"Pity, because that's all John Bellfield talks about, him and my ex could bore people to death, it's no wonder he's a manager of a crematorium!"

Chapter Six

That evening I went to a small theatre in the centre of town advertising the magician and his apprentice. There was a reasonable sized audience, a group of school children, aged around twelve or thirteen years old. Lights were lowered and the curtains opened showing various gadgets on stage. The young assistant was first on doing an assortment of card tricks and pulling flags and banners out of boxes. The children seemed to enjoy the show, even though I was bored stiff, then, on came the magician his huge form filling the small stage. But he was a professional entertainer, unlike his assistant and he performed an amazing vanishing trick, plus a levitation act that was as good as anything I have ever seen – however, not being a fan of magic, I was only too pleased to get out into the night air and head home for a good night's sleep.

That night I went to bed full of the day's activities. Lazlo Varga was an amazing character, not only was he a hypnotist he was also a very fine magician, making people disappear and to top it all he worked at the local crematorium also making bodies disappear, I lay awake making notes, until finally I fell asleep.

Next morning I decided to visit the crematorium and interview this manager Mister John Bellfield, I looked up the phone number; spoke to the manager and introduced myself, and we made an appointment for that afternoon.

I went into the Black Horse pub for a light lunch before going to my meeting, a pretty young woman was at the bar and I said in a roundabout way that she was a pleasant change from the lady that had served me yesterday…
"That's the landlord's wife, or ex-wife as she insists on being called, there was one hell of a row between her and her husband here in the pub late last night" she said pouring me a glass of red wine, "they almost came to blows."
"What was that all about?" I said.
"Evidently he, the landlord, has a young mistress, and he wants her to move in and run the pub."
"Crikey!" I said, "It's no wonder there was a row!"
"I'll say" said the pretty young woman. "He said he is going to <u>chuck</u> her out if she doesn't pack up and leave of her own accord!"

Chapter Seven

I arrived at the crematorium for my interview, a well turned out place for what it actually did, a pleasant elegant atmosphere, showing great respect for the occasion of any funeral service. John Bellfield was a pleasant man, small in stature, smartly dressed in a dark suit with white collar, waistcoat and sombre coloured tie. His office was warm with wooden walls and soft lighting. He sat behind a large tidy leather topped desk with a spotlessly clean white blotting pad and a Montblanc fountain pen neatly lined up alongside a silver letter opener.

We talked of his activities and I was allowed to make notes. He said that this crematorium had recently become privately owned, and no he was not at liberty to say by whom – but that it was well financed. Also he proudly announced that it, [the crematorium] was now heating the local swimming pool next door.

I mentioned the name Lazlo Varga being employed here…
"A fine man" said John Bellfield, "we are very lucky to have him and his assistant."
"I understand that he and his young assistant actually dispose of the bodies in the ovens." I said.
The manager silently moved his Montblanc pen from one side of his blotting pad to the other, and

quietly said "that is their position here at the crematorium – yes! We don't use names here; we all go by numbers, as do our clients. Names are only entered in our memorial book for remembrance, but we only dispose of numbers. Then when the ashes are gathered and put into jars the number is on the jar and also next to the clients name in the book, that way there is no unfortunate mix-up, if you get my meaning."

"Excellent" I said, "During a conversation I had with Lazlo and his assistant he [Lazlo] mentioned a *special* arriving. What would that be? What exactly is a *special*?"

There was silence, he stood up, and the Montblanc pen was moved again from one side to the other, followed by… "And no, I am not at liberty to discuss anything further, the interview is now at an end" and he held out his hand, I stood up, shook hands and left the building.

I walked awhile, and went into a local park and sat down on a bench watching ducks swimming and fishing in a small lake, it gave me time to think and digest what I had just witnessed. I came to the conclusion, that apart from pub gossip the only way I could further my interest in the 'goings on' in that place was through Lazlo's assistant, he liked his booze and he had a very loose tongue, he was to be my target!

Chapter Eight

I found out his name was Carlo from the pretty barmaid Julia at the Black Horse pub. She told me Carlo was a regular and a heavy drinker, which could be a problem at times particularly with the young male customers, and no, she had never had problems with him and didn't think she ever would.

I had my usual glass of wine and I ordered a cold chicken salad in a basket.

Julia the pretty barmaid wondered why the Mrs had not arrived, "tonight is usually a busy night at the Black Horse because we have live music, besides, I've found her earring at the foot of the stairway at the rear entrance. I had to go out back to get a case of wine" said Julia, "and look…" She handed a gold distinctive earring to me "Yes" I said, "that's hers, she lost it the other night on the floor where you are standing behind the bar, I left her looking for it" I said.

"I'll give it to her when she turns up" said Julia, "I hope she turns up. Look out; here comes Carlo now, good thing I brought that case of wine in! Hello Carlo!" she shouted, and holding up a bottle of wine, and picking down a wine glass from the rack, "are you staying for a glass" she said to him.

"Keep that bottle handy" he said, "pour me a glass, I'm just going to the loo!"

I waved hello by raising my glass, and he shouted "we need to talk! Don't go away!"
"I won't" I said.

Before Carlo returned I gave Julia a five pound note, "that's for you" I said, "all you have to do is fill my wine glass with that kola" I said pointing. "Let him drink as much wine as he wants – but serve me kola! I want to keep a clear head, I've got an interview to do – is that clear?"
"You journalists are a crafty lot" said Julia, "but okay, and thanks for the tip! I need every penny believe me." And she moved along the bar as the pub filled with customers for music night – live music.

Carlo returned from the loo and drank the wine waiting at the bar and reached for the bottle.
"Carlo" I said, "what's the chance of you showing me where you work?"
"I thought you saw it this afternoon?" he said knocking back the wine.
"Yes I was there" I said, "but only in the manager's office. My editor wants me to find out where the real workers spend their time, and the skill it entails" I lied, "that's you and Lazlo. The manager tells me those ovens of yours heat the swimming pool next door, how's that done?"

"No problem old chap" he said, "I can give you a full guided tour, are you or your editor paying for our wine?"

"On the house" I said, "you just help yourself, I'll put it on expenses."

Chapter Nine

During the chat I approached the question of numbers. "John the manager told me you all had numbers, not names."

"True" said Carlo, "the new owners came up with that system, it works well, my number is 2071 and Lazlo is 2072. We are always addressed as numbers when we are contacted to receive a special from the city. The special also has a number" he said. "Where's that girl, that barmaid, we need another bottle."

I waved her back from down the bar and pointed at the bottle, she waved back and made her way past customers anxious to be served, "I don't understand it" she said, "the Mrs still hasn't turned up, I've had to phone the governor and he said he was on his way in and he's also got extra help."

"That'll be his tarty girlfriend" said Carlo taking the bottle out of Julie's hand, "they are a couple from now on."

"How do you mean, from now on?" I said.

Carlo tapped the side of his nose and downed another full glass in one go.

"Do you know where the landlady is?" I asked.

"I need the loo" he said "and repeated, I need a piss" and gave a large disgusting burp and staggered off to the loo.

"Here comes the governor" said Julia, "just in time, the band has arrived!"

"I never did get my chicken salad in a basket" I said.

"Oh my God! I'm sorry" she said, "now you'll want your five quid back!"

"No matter" I said, "I'm too busy dealing with this peace of shit at the moment, besides I've lost my appetite."

"You realise he's already drunk two bottles of wine?" Julia said, "Look at the state of him now; he drank one bottle at lunchtime."

"Right" said Carlo as he returned, picking up another glass of red, "when do you want to do this tour of my lovely warm work place? You name it and I'm ready to go, anytime."

"Anytime" I said sipping the glass of kola Julia handed me.

"This lot on that stage are crap" said Carlo, waving his arm and spilling his drink. "Rap, crap" he shouted, "rubbish rap crap" he repeated.

The guvnor came forward telling him to keep it down or leave… "You can't talk to 2071 like that!" he said poking the landlord in the chest – mister 3475."

"For God sake man, go and sober up and shut that loose mouth of yours. I'm going to phone John" said the landlord.

"Don't bother, both me and the scribe here," pointing to me "are leaving!" And he looked me in the eye and tapped the side of his nose again.

I paid Julia the bill for the drinks, then we left the Black Horse pub, got into my car and we drove across town towards the crematorium.

Chapter Ten

We arrived at the crematorium around ten thirty, "are you sure I'm not getting you into trouble?" I said, "It's a bit late visiting this place."
"Night time is the best time" said Carlo as he almost fell out of my car, "just you follow me, I've got the keys to this place in case a 'special' arrives, they can arrive anytime you know" he said putting his arm around my shoulder, anytime" he repeated, "night or fucking day" and he let out a loud brewers belch and pushed a key into a large heavy iron door. "Fire proof!" he belched, banging his fist against the door.

We entered a very large room, at the far end there was what looked like five or six ovens, on the left were three four wheeled trolleys for transporting bodies. The lights in the ceiling were all caged and the floor was wall to wall with white floor tiles, all in all, not a place I would like to linger in for long, on the right hand wall was another iron door.
"What's in there?" I said walking over to it.
"Scrapings in pots" he said.
"Scrapings?" I queried.
"The body remains; ashes! We put them into numbered pots after we scrape out the ashes" he said. "Of course we sort through them first, you would be amazed at what we find," he hiccupped.
"Such as?" I said, getting out my note book.

"Orthopaedic implants, knee joints, hip joints, gold teeth, various heart gadgets, all recyclable metal items, implants for scrap." Then making a sign with a thumb and finger, "money! money! money!" he grinned.

"Of course our beloved manager gets permission first, or so he says, he thinks the money goes to a charity!"
"Well" I said "Does it?"
I got no answer as he picked up a grey bowl, "look at this lot" he said, "all good stuff!" His mobile phone rang, so loud, it made me jump.
"Lazlo!" he shouted and turned away – just as I was looking into the bowl with my eyes fixed on a single earring – I recognised it immediately and put down my note book and reached for my phone while Carlo's back was turned, I took two or three photographic shots of the earring and managed to hide my phone back into my pocket as Carlo turned picking up the grey bowl and putting it back on a table containing numbered jars.
"Was that from a recent cremation" I said trying to act normal.
"Yes, that one" he said tapping a numbered jar, "why do you…" he belched again, "…ask."
"Just curious how quickly you dispose of the pieces" I said shrugging.
"We clear as we go" he said, "talking of going, you had better sod off before Lazlo arrives, we've got a special!"

I made a quick mental note of the jar he tapped and couldn't wait to get outside on my own and write it into my note book, 3984.

Chapter Eleven

I didn't get much sleep that night, so much was going on in my head, I knew that earring belonged to the buxom blonde landlady of the Black Horse pub, and the other earring, Julia the pretty young barmaid had found at the foot of the stairs, at the back entrance of the Black Horse pub. Then there was the terrible row she spoke of the night before, all about her so called ex-husband wanting to replace his ex-wife with his mistress… but there was no getting away from that jar of ashes jar number 3984 it <u>must</u> be her ashes. He will, he decided go back to the crematorium and look at that remembrance book in the manager's office.

Next morning I had a quick coffee and cornflakes and went to the crematorium arriving at ten o'clock anxious to talk to the manager, John Bellfield. I was shown into his palatial office, the first thing I did was take a look in *that* book. I went down the list and came to the number 3984, there was no name, just the two letters, SP obviously meaning special.

The manager John Bellfield came in and we shook hands, he didn't say much, just how nice to see you again, he had a glazed look about him.
I asked "why is there no name next to number 3984?"

"It's the new management" he said, "all above board; now, what brings you back to my office?"
As he once again arranged the objects on his desk.
"It concerns someone I know who is now missing and I have reason to believe…" suddenly the door of the office opened and the huge frame of Lazlo Varga came in.
"What's he doing here?" he said pointing at me.
"It seems he is concerned about a missing person" said the manager.
"Well you don't come to a crematorium" said Lazlo, "you go to a police station. Who is this missing person?"
I said "the landlady of the pub, you know her. You were talking to her two nights ago."
"Have you asked her ex-husband if <u>he</u> knows where she is?" he said.
"No I hadn't but I have other reasons to be concerned."
"Well I can't stand about here gossiping, I have work to do and I have another show to prepare for on Saturday night, and no assistant."
"Is he sick?" I said. "He drinks far too much."
"No, it's me who is sick" said Lazlo, "sick to death of him."
"Quite so" said the manager, "he no longer works here and we have a replacement coming down from London. He left for Exeter this morning, he was very unreliable, and I do believe he was in the building last night – late last night we have rules about that!"

"Quite right" I said, "he could be very unpleasant in his cups [he was drunk]. Thank you for putting up with me on a second visit" I said, "only to be honest I want to bring my notes up to date."

"I see" said the manager, "if I can help…"

"Well" I said, "you tell me you are privately owned, but refuse to tell me who."

"I can't tell you precisely" he said.

"Just think on the lines of M15 – and you won't be far wrong."

"So it's a government ownership, state owned." I said writing it down in my note book.

"That is *not* what I said, I said think along those lines – nothing else. And that's my final word on the matter, and the Montblanc pen changed sides on the blotter again.

"You have been very helpful" I said, "incidentally, can I ask, have you ever been hypnotised?"

"Not to my knowledge" he answered, "why do you ask such a question?"

"No reason, and just one more thing" I said "that memorial book, is the number 3984 with no accompanying name the last entry?"

"I believe so" he said, getting up from his desk and turning the page of the memorial book. "NO there is one more, a special, no name of course, just the number…"

"What number is that?" I asked, pen poised…

"2071" came the answer.

"Fucking hell!" I shouted.

"I beg your pardon!" said the manager staring at me.

"Err the time" I stuttered looking at my watch, "I've just seen the time, I must go, *deadlines* I have to meet *deadlines*!

Chapter Twelve

2071 of course, was Carlo's number, first 3894, the landlord's ex-wife's number, and now Carlo, my God! It's a completely organised disappearing act, and I'm convinced that manager has been has been hypnotised, he really is in another world; nothing seems to sink in to that dull brain of his. I need a drink! I went to the Black Horse pub and ordered a bottle of red wine from Julia the pretty barmaid, who was now being ordered around by a youngish black haired handsome woman of around thirty eight to forty. The landlord's mistress was now in charge of the establishment with an iron bejewelled fist, [a ring on almost every finger]... Once I had drunk half way down my bottle of red wine, I began to relax a little, I knew that I must <u>first</u> talk to my editor before I published what I had discovered and then inform the police. Yes I know! The police should come first, but then I <u>am</u> a reporter and Fleet Street is in my blood – along with half a bottle of red wine, so publish and be damned! Is the old fashioned way to go, not first check ones list of do's and don'ts of European left-wing clap-trap, can't do this, can't do that! Give me the freedom of the press and a pen any day!

I was just pouring the dregs of my wine bottle into my empty glass, when in walked Lazlo Varga, with the kiss of death expression on his face.

He came and stood alongside me at the bar and ordered a drink, asking me to have another bottle which I declined.

I gave a large addressed envelope to Julia, asking her to post it; it was addressed to my editor and for his attention only. I followed the envelope and put a twenty pound note into Julia's pretty hands, "that's to cover the cost, and here is another twenty pounds for yourself" I said.
"Thank you kind sir" she said, mocking a curtsy, "it shall be done, but pray tell me – I don't even know your name?"

Lazlo Varga put his giant hand down on the brown addressed package saying "he doesn't have a name, he has a *number* – 3957" he said.

The End

The Stalker
By Peter Maddocks

Chapter One

Oscar Von Hagen, whose real name was Barry Fenton, was an ex fleet street journalist and latter day artist just turned sixty four, and moved to Spain several years ago leaving an ex-wife back in England.

He started every day the same, at Bar Rosa, in the centre of the village where he rented a small but comfortable villa on the edge of town. He had a few man friends and the occasional woman friend, but nothing serious as he enjoyed his own company. He exchanged banter in broken Spanish with his Andalucían neighbours, life for him was easy, the wine was red and the sun was warm, although sometimes he swore there were two Fridays in a week, time was catching up with him.

One morning at Bar Rosa, he had collected his morning English newspaper from the newsagent across the street, and was just about to settle down for a read while he waited for coffee when an attractive woman waved a car away from the curb, turned and fell over the small menú del día sign, showing the price of today's lunch. The contents of her handbag spilt over the floor, Oscar Von Hagen quickly helped her to her feet, while Maria the waitress collected everything from the handbag. The woman dusted herself down with embarrassment; Oscar asked if she was hurt…

"Only my pride!" she answered thanking him for his concern.

"Sit down" he said, and called to Maria for two coffees and two brandies.

"Oh no!" said the woman "far too early for brandy."

"My dear lady" said the ex-journalist, "take it from one who knows, it is <u>never</u> too early for a brandy in Spain. Well not in this village anyway!"

The hand bag was returned intact with thanks and the coffee and brandy arrived at the table.

"Mind if I join you?" said Oscar "you can sit alone if you wish" he said pointing himself to another table.

"No, do join me please" she said, "I've just waved my husband off to his golf; we're here for a three week golf tournament. Well <u>he</u> is!" she added, "I'm just a golf widow, but I intend to enjoy the break despite my ungainly entrance."

"It could happen to anyone" said Oscar. "I've warned Juan, the owner of this establishment about that damned menú del día sign being too low on the ground. Now perhaps he will listen."

She sipped her brandy "you are right" she said, "brandy and bruises do go together."

"You are bruised?" asked Oscar showing concern.

"No, just joking" she said, "and isn't this coffee good?"

"Best part of the day" said Oscar, "Coffee, brandy and now a very beautiful woman!"

She ignored his remark and said "are you visiting Spain?"

"No; hell no!" he repeated, "I live here, have done for years…"

The polite conversation continued for well over an hour… "I must go" she said looking at her watch. "I want to go to the bank; I am determined to get some shopping in Marbella before I go back."

"What do you go back to?" said Oscar with a smile.

"Oh to our beautiful country pub in the Cotswolds" she said, "I love it, it's hard work, but it's also our home."

"Do you own or lease?" said Oscar.

"Oh we are the owners my dear" she said boastfully, "my husband is a professional golfer as well as a publican, his family have been publicans for years, no amateur is he, either at golf or in a pub. I must go…" she stood up, dusting herself down. She was tall, almost as tall as he was and as she bent dusting her blue skirt, Oscar caught sight of her full breasts hiding behind a crisp white blouse, half unbuttoned. She suddenly looked at him with her green eyes wide open, aware that he was filling his thoughts with her body. And she stood upright and adjusted her blouse.

"Should we meet again" she said, "I promise to make a better entrance than I did this morning, most unladylike, thanks for saving my life, I'll get the coffee and the brandy" she took her purse from her handbag, as if to pay the bill…

"Over my dead fleet street body" said Oscar standing up, "men pay for drinks where I come from!"

"Then I will not dent your masculine pride" she said, "thank you."

"Will I – we, see you again?" said Oscar.

"Why not" she said "this is Spain and I am on holiday!" then with a wave, she left.

Oscar slumped back into his regular seat; he could still smell her perfume. Maria the waitress wiped his table and collected the empty glasses.

"Another brandy "he said without looking up. Maria gave him a knowing look and kicked up her leg as she moved away, "make it a large one!" he shouted after her.

Later that day when he returned to his villa the thoughts of his encounter with the woman disturbed him. He must see her again he thought, I should have asked where she was staying. A villa? A hotel? He made visual sketches of her from memory on his sketchpad… pity I haven't a photograph he thought, a likeness in pencil would make a fine conversational piece on our next meeting – I must see her again – I must!

Chapter Two

Next morning Oscar was at a table outside Bar Rosa, the warm sun was up and he ordered his coffee and brandy, and waited... watching every car that passed, expecting it to stop and the fine figure of a woman step out and greet him with a knowing smile. No such luck, the morning passed.
"No newspaper today?" asked Maria "no beautiful woman either" she said smiling.
"I'm going to get my paper now" he said, "you just get me another brandy and mind your own business!" he said tapping the side of his nose.

His day passed in a low mood despite a cloudless sky and a head dazed by brandy. Stupid man he thought, "stupid elderly man" he said to himself.

Next morning he picked up his paper first, before he crossed the road to the bar, when, as he waited for the morning traffic to clear... he saw her – she was already sitting alone at a table, he almost ran across the road through the traffic and greeted her with a breathless "hello again!"
"Hello" she said, "I didn't fall over today, I managed to avoid that menú del día sign" she said pointing.
"May I join you" he said, about to sit down.
"Be my guest" she said, "but the coffee and brandy are on me today, I'll just have coffee."

"Splendid" said Oscar, waving to Maria the waitress.

"We never got round to names the other day? My name is Oscar" he said offering his hand, "Oscar Von Hagen."
"What a splendid name" she said, "I'm Olivia, Mrs Olivia Bradshaw."
"Such a beautiful name" Oscar said, "where are you staying by the way!"
Olivia said "We are at the hotel on the edge of town."
"La Rueda?" said Oscar.
"That's it" she said.
"Ah, here's our coffee, and my brandy. Your husband golfing today?" asked Oscar.
"Oh yes, as I said, it's a tournament. I'll get no attention from him while that's on" she said.
"That's a pity" said Oscar, sipping his brandy. "Why don't I show you the town?"
"What's there to see?" she replied.
"The famous falls" he said, "and then there are the mountains…" he waved his hand to the sky.
"Maybe another day" she said, "I'm off to Marbella with a friend today, to spend some of my euros. Look!" she held up her handbag with both hands.
"A man friend?" he mocked "and you a married woman."

"A <u>lady</u> friend" she answered "another golf widow, there are hundreds of us golf widows you know. I'm meeting her in half an hour; here… she has a car."

"I see" said Oscar, looking back at Maria the waitress who was pulling mocking faces.

They both drank their coffees until a blue Renault Clio pulled up outside the bar. "This is my lift" she said, going over to the bar to pay for the drinks, and with a 'lovely to see you again' and fleeting wave… was gone!

Oscar watched her body as she got into the car, and he noted the number plate on the paper tablecloth as the two women drove away.

"Made a date yet?" asked Maria, as Oscar tore off the number he had written on the tablecloth and stuffed it in his pocket.

"Mind your own business!" he said and picked up his paper and made his way to his car parked up the hill. He knows that the shopping centre is easily accessible just before you drive into Marbella. The only problem is the car park is large and finding a blue Clio there won't be easy. But find it he must and park as near to it as possible.

Chapter Three

The trip to Marbella through the mountains is always pleasurable, even when you have a woman on your mind, the winding road the changing colours and the sudden sight of the Mediterranean, not to mention seeing the African coastal mountains on the other side – even a glimpse of Gibraltor can stir an English heart.

Oscar turned into the retail car park, hundreds of cars… "Pick a parking lane and drive up it!" he said out loud, not this one, try the next, there's a Clio, no its green, keep going, up this one, there's a space, I'll try on foot he thought. He parked, locked his car, noted exactly where he was and in the next but one lane *was* a blue Clio, he gets his scrap of tablecloth note from his trouser pocket, yes, that's it! That is the very car Olivia got into. Now – do I wait here? Or do I go into the shopping centre? Well he thought I can at least stand around the entrance, better still there is a coffee bar where I can watch the entrance from, so that he did. He sat down, ordered coffee and kept his eyes on the entrance as people of all shapes and sizes came and went into those sliding doors. He put his phone in front of him, with the camera application activated… and waited.

An hour passed, and suddenly, there she was with a girlfriend as she said, both carrying carrier bags full of goods from the various stores, as they came closer he aimed his phone and took pictures. She turned and caught a glimpse of him with his phone, but the traffic cleared and her friend grabbed her arm and pulled her across the road leading into the car park.

Oscar waited and having paid for his coffee went back to his vehicle, he unlocked the car and got in – but as he was about to close the door, having secured his seat belt, the face of Olivia appeared, she held his car door open and looked in…
"Are you following me?!" she said in a serious commanding voice.
"Following?" Oscar repeated, "hell no! But hello! – what are you doing here?" he said in all innocence.
"I told you at Bar Rosa 'I'm shopping with a girlfriend, now, what's your excuse?"
"Excuse? What do you mean excuse?" Oscar repeated, "No excuse, I came to meet a friend on business."
"I saw no friend Oscar" she said, "I just saw you at the café with a phone in your hand."
"Exactly" said Oscar lying, "I'm just off to meet him at a bar along the beach."
Olivia said nothing more, she just slammed shut his car door and walked away –

Oscar started the car, put it in reverse and back out, changed into first gear and looked around for Olivia, she had gone, so he had to drive off and leave her to her friend. That was close he thought, but I think I got away with it!

That evening, Oscar having returned home, poured himself a drink, and with the aid of a magnifying glass studied the photograph he had taken of Olivia with his phone. He made several sketches of her face and when he was convinced he had her likeness he prepared to paint her portrait.

Chapter Four

Oscar spent five hours that evening painting in acrylic on canvas, he finally put his brush down and studied what he had done, not bad, although she had a rather concerned serious look, not unlike what he saw when she confronted him at the car door! However, it was a good likeness. He had captured her mane of red brown hair, and her green eyes, he was pleased he had got them right and she looked straight at him – one of those that follow you around the room pictures you can't escape. Her eyes, they looked at you and through you, yes, he was pleased with what he had achieved he thought as he cleaned his brushes.

Next morning he showered and dressed and studied the picture he had painted the night before. It pleased him, he had captured that certain look, he thought she was quite beautiful, I must see her this morning, and what time is it?

He arrived at the paper shop and checked his post in the box he rents, crossed the road and settled down at his usual table at the bar, Maria the waitress arrived with his coffee and brandy, an hour went by and so did another coffee and another brandy.
"She won't be coming today" Maria said. "You must have frightened her away with your tongue hanging out" she laughed.

"Mind your own business" he shouted throwing loose change on the table, he folded his newspaper and left heading up the hill to his car.

He decided to check out the hotel she said she was staying at; maybe he would see her, if only from the car… he parked close to the entrance of La Rueda hotel and waited. After an hour or so he got out of the car and locked it, and went into the hotel lounge and sat in a comfortable chair and waited, the desk clerk kept looking over at him and eventually asked if he was waiting for someone and could he help?
"Yes" said Oscar, "A Mrs Olivia Bradshaw, I believe the lady and her husband are staying here, for the golf tournament!"
The clerk moved back to his desk and checked the register… "I am sorry Mr & Mrs Bradshaw checked out this morning sir."
"That can't be" said Oscar standing up, "he's playing in the golf tournament!"
"Well he probably didn't make the cut!" the desk clerk said. "They left and went to stay in Marbella I believe."
Oscar said nothing and walked out.

He got to his car and looked back, she had gone, and all he had now was the portrait. He drove back avoiding the police who were stopping cars at the roundabouts; they would smell the brandy on his breath.

He stripped off once back indoors, he showered for almost an hour, cleaning the anger from his body, the stench of eau de cologne, after shave and stupidity of a man of his age being possessed by a woman, someone else's woman! He dried himself, put on a dressing gown, picked up the portrait put it into a black plastic bag and dumped it in the <u>bin</u> out next to his garage door. "I'm clean" he said to himself as he sat watching a film on television called Dorian Grey. "Rubbish!" he shouted and switched it off, then he went into the bathroom took a sleeping tablet and went to bed.

Things will look better in the morning he thought, pulling the bed covers over his head and sleep overtook him...

Chapter Five

Next morning he woke up dying for a pee and jumped out of bed and into the bathroom still half asleep, he lifted the lid of the loo, and fumbled for his penis, he tried again, nothing, no penis could he find!!! Even when he put his hand between his legs, then suddenly he was aware of a mass of hair hanging around his shoulders, red brown hair, and his chest bulged beneath the vest he had slept in, he put both hands on his chest, it moved, he had breasts! He leaned across to the large mirror over his sink only to see not himself – but the mirror image of her.... Olivia looking back at him! "What the hell!" he shouted, not in his voice, it was in her voice, the person standing almost naked in his bathroom was Olivia Bradshaw, that woman he had dreamed of being this close to, was him! "I'm still me inside" he shouted prodding his temple with her finger, and in her voice, "I'm me! Yet I'm her! I must get dressed" he said.

Then as he went into the bedroom and slid back the sliding door of his wardrobe he turned and looked again at the image reflected in his full length mirror standing in the corner of his bedroom, I'm a bloody woman, not a bloody man – no – "I'm a bloody freak!" he shouted, I can't wear my own clothes what the hell can I put on? I can't go out like this! "Patricia" he said, Patricia the ex-wife left clothes here, in the wardrobe of the other bedroom, he went into the other wardrobe and found some female clothes on hangers at the far end. I can still wear my own underpants and vest underneath he thought, let's try this denim dress? No! Then he spotted a pair of women's jeans on the floor, he tried them on and they fitted, clinging to his/her legs like silk stockings! I can now just wear any shirt he thought, shoes? Not even going to try high heels, flat sandals, that'll do me, he stood looking at him or I should say herself in the mirror. My god! He thought, I fancy myself, I'm having sexual thoughts about my own reflection, and "it's bloody crazy" he/she screamed. "What do I do now?"

He went back into the bathroom and splashed cold water on his face, thank goodness she has perfect skin, he thought, no need for make-up, I can't imagine painting my face with make-up, cock-up more like if I tried that!

Now, I've got to go out, I can't lock myself away; besides, I will need cash soon, hell! He thought my cash and credit cards! Don't tell me they've changed, he gathered his wallet from his coat pocket and checked its contents, phew, no, they haven't changed, "at least I have money" he said out loud in her voice. But it will have to be the hole in the wall, I'm somebody else like this, how did this happen?

Looking down at his shapely desirable body, fortunately, the weather is warm so I can go out, "I'll have to buy a coat or a jacket" he said picking up his car keys. He opened his door and took a deep breath and walked out into a sunny Spanish morning.

He/she, was about to get into his car parked at the end of his drive when Alfredo his next door neighbour called from the lane outside his villa... "Hola" and in Spanish asked after Señor Oscar, "where is he?" he shouted.

Realising he was getting into Oscars car and he was a she, Olivia, not Oscar, she answered in perfect Spanish "I took him to the airport this morning, early, he has gone to Barcelona, I am house sitting for him, until he returns!" he lied.
"Okay" waved Alfredo and moved on.

Oscar was quite proud of his quick thinking excuse for not being around. At least it gave him time to work things out, and cope with his ridiculous situation.

Chapter Six

He drove his car out of the lane and onto the motorway, he would make his way through the mountains to the Marbella shopping centre where he/she, could blend in, not known to anyone! I can't go into the village like this!

He arrived within twenty five minutes from where he lived, easy drive, not a lot of traffic and no rotundas [roundabouts] for police to stand on and call you in to check your documents, documents in someone else's name, however here in Spain your car insurance covers the car, not the person, so although he was safe insurance wise, 'she' had no documents, no drivers licence, nothing! <u>No way</u> could he produce his own licence looking like a woman he thought.

He made his way into the shopping centre, very aware that he/she was attracting attention from young men, having a t-shirt on with no bra was not a good look for a woman with these beautiful breasts! I must buy a coat of some sort and cover myself up, I'm attracting too much attention in tight jeans and a loose shirt, being a man inside a woman's body, the first shop he thought of was a major well known British department store, not one of the many off beat dress and shoe shops that would normally catch a woman's eye in Marbella. So the UK store is was, and he found a jacket that matched her colouring, *he* thought, although the young woman who served him queried the purchase, by checking that she was serving the right customer standing in line to be served...

Once outside he decided to have a coffee, but first he must put the jacket on, and without thinking walked into the gents' toilet marked caballero! Only to be stopped by a couple of laughing young men about to unzip their trousers! He/she realising his mistake quickly backed out and sheepishly went into the ladies, and finding the privacy of the toilet cubicle put the jacket on after removing the labels... then a brief look in the mirror he made his escape to one of the many and varied nationality restaurants in the food hall, he chose a coffee bar and found an empty table at the back, ordering a bacon and tomato bocadillo and a coffee. Again, more man food than woman, but he was hungry and just about to tuck in when he spotted a familiar face... HER face, Olivia, my god! Of course that hotel clerk said she and her husband had gone to a Marbella hotel. He must leave, quickly, before their eyes could meet. He turned away and finished his coffee, wrapped what was left of the bocadillo in a napkin and went to the till to pay, keeping his back to the *real* Olivia Bradshaw and her husband who were in deep conversation. He then realised he must get well clear of Marbella, far too risky, and made his/her way back to the car.

On the journey back he finished eating what was left of the bocadillo, able to eat like a man who was hungry in the privacy of a car, now covered in breadcrumbs. He needed money from the hole in the wall, he now had to chance going into the village to get the cash and purchase enough food to keep him indoors, away from enquiring eyes, for at least a week, until he can come to terms with his new identity… he had to go, he had no choice!

Next day he took a chance at visiting the village, unfortunately the bank with the hole in the wall was right next door to the bar he used every morning, but he *had* to chance it, he must have money.

The machine was free of people as he approached it, and he/she put in his card and punched in his pin number, he waited and money appeared, and he stuffed it in the pocket of the jacket he had purchased yesterday, as he turned to leave there was Maria, the waitress, waving to him/her, from a table at Bar Rosa.

She shouted in Spanish "have you seen Señor Oscar? We are very worried he never misses his morning coffee and brandy, never!!"
She could not ignore Maria's remarks, she had to walk over to her and make conversation. "No" he/she said, "my husband and I have moved to Marbella, I'm just here to use my bank, we are

about to return to England! Perhaps he's gone to Barcelona." This he thought would tie in with what he had told his neighbour Alfredo should Maria see him.

"I'm *sure* he would have told <u>me</u> he was going to Barcelona" Maria said reluctantly, "I'm sure he would have told me" she repeated. "Can I get you a coffee Señora?"

"No" Oscar said "I must get back to my husband, we leave this evening" and he turned away and left to get back to the car before anyone else he knew should turn up, he had bought a good weeks' worth of food shopping, now in the boot of his car, so there would be no need for him to leave the villa and risk being recognised as the woman at the bar who had talked to Oscar the last couple of mornings before he disappeared!

Chapter Seven

Almost a week passed by without mishap he/she had kept well away from people but still he, Oscar Von Hagen was trapped in the body of the beautiful Olivia Bradshaw.

It was on Saturday morning that two local policemen came to the door; they had received a report about a missing person, Oscar Von Hagen, known at this address, "can we ask who you are Señora? Señorita?"
"Yes of course" she answered; "I am Olivia Von Hagen, Oscar Von Hagen's sister" she lied.
"Can we see your passport?" said the police officer with a clipboard of papers.
"I'm afraid I have no identification" she lied again, "I flew here from Barcelona, I arrived and left my handbag on the bus from the airport, and nothing as yet has been handed in, I am constantly on the phone to them! So I can't prove my identity at the moment."
"You speak perfect Spanish" said the police officer, "what is your nationality?"
"I'm from the Netherlands" she said.
"There was a silence as the policeman made notes, and then he said "you must come with us to the station, until we can prove your identity."
And a second policeman took the arm of Olivia and led her to the police car. Oscar knew that he had talked himself into a tight corner, one that he

was going to have great difficulty to get out of! "My tablets!" she said suddenly, "I'm a diabetic and I <u>must</u> have my tablets."

"Where are they?" said the policeman with the clipboard.

They enter the villa and Oscar goes to the bathroom cupboard and opens it "Oh no! I forgot!" she said "I took my prescription to the farmacia yesterday, they are in my car, and I'll need my keys!" Oscar picks up the car keys and goes out to the car, opens it and gets into the driving seat quickly inserting the key, "I put them in my locker here" she said reaching towards the door – "here they are!" she said… and started the car, slammed the car door as the policeman tried to grab the door handle, Oscar took off in a cloud of dust as the rear wheels spun on the gravel, the policeman with the chipboard dropped it and jumped to stop the speeding vehicle, all too late… Oscar was flat out though the hedge of young pine trees, and off down the lane, onto the motorway and raced off with his/her foot to the floor with the accelerator, knowing the police have means to catch someone fleeing by car other than chasing them, he decided quickly to go to his friend Eric who had a workshop at the local poligino [industrial estate] some five kilometres along the highway. Eric's store, with gaping open doors, always open to view his second hand furniture… if I can make it, and get inside, off the road…

I'll be safe thought Oscar, just for a while until I gather my wits about me. He turned sharp left into the poligino, long lines, almost a maze of workshops and cars, this is the one thought Oscar, thank God its open! And he skidded and braked as he entered the mouth of the workshop and came to a standstill in the dark, right at the back between two piles of second hand furniture!

Chapter Eight

He/she opened the car door and jumped out and hid amongst the chairs and tables, looking though the dark at the gaping open doorway for any sign of movement, nothing! No people, no cars, no police. Oscar pulled down a chair and sat on it waiting, making sure nothing was happening out there in the daylight, she looked at her watch; it was coffee drinking time, that's where everybody will be, in the bar around the corner! Now what shall I do next? Thought Oscar, I can't ask Eric for help, dressed like this; he wouldn't know me from Adam – or Eve!

Back at the villa there is much activity; police are going from room to room, checking everything, books, clothes, draws, all the cupboards, and outside to the bins, particularly the one with the black plastic bag containing a portrait of Olivia. The now fugitive, Olivia, wanted for questioning about identity and the whereabouts of the missing Oscar Von Hagen, and claiming to be his sister.

The policeman in charge of the investigation inside the villa is shown the portrait of the beautiful Olivia found outside in the bin, wrapped in a black plastic bag! He studies the portrait as he walks out into the sunshine to his car radio to call the local station. As he talks describing what had been found, he places the painting, face up on top of his police car, just as another police officer calls him back into the villa.

Leaving the painting on top of the police car in the blazing sun, the beautiful face of Olivia fades, almost melting into the canvas, when the police officer returns to continue describing the painting over the car radio, he takes the picture off of the roof of the car, only to find that the beautiful Olivia had changed into the face of a man with grey white hair!

Chapter Nine

And in the warehouse workshop in the poligino, sitting behind a pile of second hand tables and sitting on a chair, was a man with grey white hair, dressed in woman's clothing, Oscar Von Hagen had returned to his own image. He first noticed his hands were no longer the hands of a woman, his beautiful sexy breasts had gone, and so had his mane of red brown hair – he was normal again, as normal as a man can be dressed in women's clothing, he quickly got out of the denim dress, he had on his men's underpants and t-shirt, he kicked off the small sandals now crippling his feet, and stepped out from behind the tables and quickly got back into his car and reversed it out into the bright sunlight, passing a group of people walking back to their workshops.

He pulled out onto the highway and headed back to the villa, he just got to the lane leading up to it when a police officer stepped out of nowhere and with raised arms stopped the car. "Turn off the engine and step out of the car" he said, unbuttoning his side gun holster.
Oscar put his arms up and did exactly what was requested of him. "Are you the owner of this car Señor?"
"Yes I am" Oscar said, arms still above his head.
"Your name?" said the police officer now looking inside and around the car.

"Oscar Von Hagen" he replied.
"Now open the boot" said the officer pointing with one hand, the other on the handle of his firearm.
Oscar obliged, and opened the car boot – nothing! There was just a spare wheel and tools.
"Can I speak?" asked Oscar, the officer nodded.
"This is <u>my</u> car" and then pointing up the lane, "up this lane is <u>my</u> villa!"
"Lock and leave the car and walk ahead of me" said the policeman.
"I have bare feet!" said Oscar, "can we not drive up? This car will be blocking the road…"

The policeman withdrew his gun from its holster saying "you drive and I'll sit next to you" he said waving his gun in Oscars face.
Oscar obliged and steadily drove the car up the lane and into his drive, parking next to a police car.
"We've been looking for this car – where did you find it?" said the officer in charge to the policeman who stopped Oscar.
"Down the lane with this man at the wheel" said the young policeman waving his gun at Oscar.
"Put that thing away" said the man in charge, "who is he? And why is he undressed!"
"That's how he was sir" came the reply.
"Can *I* speak" said Oscar getting out of his car, "I am Oscar Von Hagen, this is my car and this…" he said waving both arms, "is <u>my</u> bloody villa! What is going on?"

The office in charge lifted up the painting, saying "is this you?"

Oscar looked closely at the picture, "yes, that's me – where did you get that?"

"In that bin!" said the officer pointing, "wrapped in a black plastic bag, but it wasn't like this when we found it."

"Well what was it like?" said Oscar.

"Never you mind" said the officer, "have you got identification?"

"Yes" he said "I have a passport in my draw in my bedroom" pointing at his home.

The officer called back towards the villa, "a man's passport – did we find one?"

"Yes sir" someone shouted from inside, and another officer appeared handing over a passport.

The man in charge studied it and said "very well, Señor Hagen, go and put some clothes on, then you have some explaining to do down at the station!"

He said to his young policeman "you found the car; you can drive it to the station yard for examination. I will take <u>him</u> in!" he said pointing back at the villa.

Chapter Ten

At the police station Oscar was interviewed "you do realise we have had officers out looking for you" said the officer in charge of the investigation. "You had been reported missing, we interviewed your sister this morning and she made a run for it in <u>your</u> car, almost knocking down one of my officers, there is a warrant out for her arrest!"
"Well" said Oscar, sitting facing the officer in charge over a bare table and under a loud clicking clock. "Well I have news for you – I <u>don't</u> have a sister, <u>never</u> had a sister. Haven't got a sister!" he repeated.
"Then how do you account for this woman calling herself your sister? Being in your villa early this morning and, by the look of her dress when she opened the door, she had been there <u>all</u> night!"
"Not with my permission" said Oscar.
"…And for her being there at all?" said the officer getting more perplexed by the minute!
"I don't" Oscar answered.
"You" said the officer calmly, "turned up this afternoon in the same car your *sister* drove off in, half dressed! That is *you* were half dressed, not your *sister*"
"For the last time" said Oscar "I do not have a bloody sister! And I found my car where I left it in the poligino."
"You left your keys in a parked car?" the officer questioned.

"I was worse for wear" he said looking away.

"You were drunk?" said the officer writing it down.

"I had been at a party, I had had a few drinks and I met this woman, and drove to a quiet spot in the poligino and I – we got into the back of the car for sex. I removed my trousers and she took off some clothes, at least I think she did" lied Oscar, "it's all a bit of a blur – next thing I know I wake up in this workshop full of furniture in my underwear, I look outside, no car, so I got a chair off a table and sat for a while and nursed a hangover!"

"Go on" said the officer still writing it all down.

"Then suddenly my car came racing into the warehouse and a rather beautiful woman jumped out, I ducked down behind tables so as not to be seen. She jumps out and starts stripping off! Next thing I know she is getting into _my_ shirt and trousers out of the back of my bloody car!"

"What then? Did you talk to her?"

"No fear!" said Oscar "I'm half naked, she's wearing my gear and driving my car, plus I'm in no condition to tackle anyone, male or female" he lied, "If you go back and look, her clothes are probably still on the floor in that warehouse" he said.

"We shall look" said the astonished officer. "Now what happened to the woman who wasn't your sister, where did she go?"

"I haven't a clue!" said Oscar lying through his teeth, "and what's more, I don't bloody care!"

"And you haven't seen her since?" said the officer. "Of course I haven't seen her" answered Oscar, "as soon as she left I got in the car and drove off to my villa – the rest you know! I was arrested by your lot" he said standing up, "can I go?"

The investigating officer put down his pen. "You can go for now, pending further enquires" he said. An English woman we contacted has claimed you were <u>stalking</u> her, in fact she has made a complaint, and there is the matter of this woman who spent the night in *your* villa, plus you say you had sex with a woman in *your* car… I would say you have a lot more explaining to do. Not to mention on that very weird portrait of the same woman in a black plastic bag, that changed into <u>YOU</u>! However for now, you are free to go. Do <u>not</u> leave the village, and we will hold on to your passport pending further enquires.

Chapter Eleven

Next morning Oscar Von Hagen went into the village and picked up a newspaper, crossed the road and sat at his usual place at Bar Rosa, Maria served him his usual coffee and brandy without saying a word.

After about an hour following the second coffee and brandy a rather attractive woman got out of a car, and waved goodbye to the driver, then turning she banged her shapely leg against the menú del día sign left by the roadside, and a little too low to be seen. The woman hopped over to Oscar's table holding her bruised leg, "that dammed sign" she said, "mind if I sit here?"
"Please, help yourself!" said Oscar Von Hagen standing up and folding his newspaper under his arm – he slowly walked away.

Maria the waitress came out to the woman asking if she was okay. "What's the matter with that miserable old devil?" said the woman looking back and rubbing her shapely bruised leg…
"Take no notice of him" said Maria, "he *was* known as Oscar Von Hagen, claimed he was an artist who painted pictures. *Now* it turns out his *real* name is Barry Fenton and he stalks women! He is now known as <u>The Stalker</u>

The End

Voices

By Peter Maddocks

Daniel Kirby.

As a little boy of five he had this imaginary friend, Benji, short for Benjamin. He would sit holding conversations with his friend, allowing gaps for him, Benji, to have his say. Then either agree or disagree with whatever he had to say.

Both Daniels' parents found it rather amusing, and almost encouraged further conversation with his imaginary friend by saying 'and what was Benji on about today Daniel?' Daniel would either respond with a very brief update or insist that it was a very private conversation!

By the age of twelve, this continued with added friends, all imaginary, and each with a distinct name, male or female. But Benji was his favourite.

Also by this time both parents tended to ignore the situation by pretending they didn't hear what Daniel had said, or by just walking away and leaving him to either talk to himself or to his imaginary friends.

On school visits for parents day, teachers would comment on what a busy family the Kirby's were, so many brothers and sisters Daniel had, not to mention all his many, bright intelligent friends, he was a credit to them for sure.

Birthday thirteen turned out to be a very unlucky number for Daniel. Even more so for his mother and father, they were killed crossing a railway line on the way back from their local pub. As Daniel was under 18 and an only child he was taken into care, the local schoolteacher when informed of the situation was amazed that he had no brothers and sisters, because of his stories about such a large family and his many friends.

After making further enquiries the authorities discovered that he had a grandmother who was very willing to care for him in her attractive three bedroomed bungalow just outside the village. Granny who turned up to collect Daniel was dressed like someone in the nineteen thirties with a matching car almost from the same period. 'A bit scatty' was a term used by the matron of the children's care home, 'but with a very loving nature,' perfect for the needs of a thirteen year old boy having been orphaned so tragically.

Granny who insisted on being addressed as Gloria, after a very famous film star from the past called Gloria Swanson, of a particular film called 'Sunset Boulevard.' "You, dear boy, will call me Gloria" she said, as they entered through the gate leading up to her bungalow. "I was an extra in a film once and the director who was very handsome, said I looked like Gloria Swanson. He said I had her eyes and her profile" turning her face sideways…

Daniel nodded in agreement, "I like the name Gloria" he said.
"Good boy" she answered, "far better than granny, very common, Grrrranny! Rolling her r's.

As they entered the bungalow, Gloria [granny], pointed to a bedroom off the hallway and said "that is to be your room Daniel, next to the toilet, boy's need to be close to a toilet as I remember."

"Do you have men friends then Gloria?" said Daniel.
"All in my head" said Gloria, "I have many friends, both male and female up here in my head" tapping her temple with her finger.
"So do I" answered Daniel, "many friends!"
"Then we shall get along fine Daniel" she said, "I'll put the kettle on…"

Daniel settled in easily, he liked living with Gloria, she was different, and she had many imaginary friends. He would hear her talking to them at night, he even knew some of their names – and so did Benji *his* imaginary friend, he told Daniel he also knew some of her friends! They were much older of course, but he was able to identify them to Daniel as he heard Gloria call them out, name by name. The little house was full of people. Loving, kind and friendly people thought Daniel, 'I'm happy living here, very happy.'

Gloria and he would go shopping together in her beautiful old fashioned car to the supermarket a mile or so down the road, Gloria would drive, missing a gear now and then. Today, as before, Daniel sat next to her. "Did my friends Hamish and Dorothy get in the back?" she said.
Daniel looked back at the empty seats, "yes" he said, "they are sitting together holding hands."
"They're lovers" she said smiling, nudging Daniels shoulder with her elbow, as she missed yet another gear.

Gloria arrived at the supermarket and parked the car in the disabled section and turned off the engine… "Go and get a trolley Daniel" she asked, "while I lock up the car, it's very valuable" she said, waiving the keys in her hand, "oh dear, go and help Dorothy, she's got her safety belt stuck in the back."
Daniel got out and opened the rear car door, "can I give you a hand Dorothy?" He said, looking into an empty seat.
"Good boy" Gloria shouted. "Once she is out, slam the door and I can lock up the car. Hamish?" she called to her other imaginary friend, "slam your door shut!"
"I'll go and get a trolley" shouted Daniel, "I'll wait for you all at the entrance, and I've got a coin!"

Gloria and Daniel met up and started shopping; Gloria had a shopping list in her hand, saying "we must concentrate Daniel. How many have you got for supper?"

"There will be three" he replied, "Benji and his girlfriend Betty."

"And my three" added Gloria, "with me, Hamish and Dorothy, that makes six. Off we go, let us shop!"

They piled the trolley with goods from the shelves as Gloria called and ticked off her list. "That's about it" she said, "except for my champagne, my guests love champagne" she repeated, "I'm quite famous for it! You young people will have a cola, help yourself Daniel, and reach me that bottle above your head – make it two bottles, plus two colas. Good boy, here, hand my card to Hamish; he likes to pay, being a man!"

Daniel took her card and held it up as if to pass it on, "Hamish says I'm to do the paying today Gloria, as I am now the man living in your house."

"As you wish" replied Gloria, "he's right, you are the man of the house now" patting him on the head. "Dorothy" she called, "you and I will go back to the car, while the men folk bring all the goodies!"

Daniel was handed the shopping list with four numbers written on the back, pin numbers for the card.

'Don't lose the card or the list' said Benji his imaginary friend, *'they are valuable commodities.'*

At the checkout as Daniel loaded the shopping back into the trolley the young lady said "your Gloria's young grandson I hear."
"Yes" answered Daniel.
"She left instructions for me to introduce myself, I'm Eileen, and I look out for the dear old lady because she tends to be a bit forgetful. Put the card in the machine, do you have her numbers? Or are you also a bit forgetful? It could run in the family" she said, leaning over in a playful whisper.

Daniel punched in the four numbers with his index finger without saying a word.
'Well done!' whispered Benji his imaginary friend, 'this could be very useful...'
Be quiet" said Daniel. Then seeing a surprised look on the shop girls' face, he said "not you Eileen, I was talking to myself."

"I said it was heredity" laughed Eileen, "your granny does exactly that. Have a good day!" she sang out as she turned to greet the next customer.

Daniel hastily arrived at the rear of the fine old car and opened the boot as an elderly man waved to him saying "that's a beautiful old car you've got there son, mint condition." Daniel slammed down the boot giving the old man half a wave and thumbs up sign...

Gloria shouted "Hamish says 'hurry up boy'. So get in the car, we're wasting fuel with this engine running, I'm not made of money." Daniel jumped in beside his grandmother as the old car jerked forward; Gloria once more missed the first gear. "Dorothy is starving, and so am I" said Gloria, "thank heavens for ready meals and a microwave. It won't be long before supper."

The car purred along the road to the bungalow having driven through two amber traffic lights and one almost red! "Here we are!" shouted Gloria, "jump out and open the gates Daniel, the sooner I park this beauty the sooner we can eat. Help Dorothy out, she's bound to have trouble with her seatbelt." Then throwing open the driver's door she shouts "thank you Hamish, you are a gentleman. Now help Daniel with retrieving the goodies from the boot."

Inside the bungalow it was warm and welcoming, with a pleasant smell from an electric air freshener, that according to Gloria, matched her perfume to perfection!

Gloria and Daniel got to work on getting supper ready, [or was it dinner?] However, Gloria was busy in the kitchen with the microwave as she stripped packing off six ready to cook meals, and lined them up to be heated, Daniel meanwhile was following Gloria's instructions by laying the table

for six. "You and I will sit at either end, and our guests will sit two either side, perfect. The candles are in the second draw of the welsh dresser..." she shouted from the kitchen. "And the matches are on the top shelf on the left."
"I've got them!" Daniel shouted back.
"Well done" she answered, "now open a bottle of champagne and serve our guests, but first bring a glass in for me, don't break anything with the flying cork when you open it. Daniel used a teacloth to stop the cork doing damage, and as it popped its exit from the bottle, Gloria applauded the sound from the kitchen.

Candles were lit, lights were turned down low, food was served for six, and glasses were topped up with champagne or cola. Soft music filled the room from somewhere in a dark corner, and Gloria and Daniel sat at each end of the table; the imaginary guests were conspicuous by their absence.

However, Gloria held conversation with six people as did Daniel. "I must say" said Gloria raising her glass, "it's good to be amongst friends..."

After a long noisy dinner party Daniel started to clear the table of uneaten food. The champagne glasses were empty, as Gloria had wandered around in deep conversation with her imaginary guests, and had scoffed the lot, consequently by now she was quite drunk, happily drunk, but of no use to Daniel in clearing up the evenings leftovers. "Our guests are about to leave" shouted Gloria, raising an empty glass and draining the dregs of the last champagne bottle half into the glass and the remains onto the floor! "Will you show them out when their taxi arrives Daniel my dear, I'm off to my bed, we can wash up the dishes in the morning, goodnight, sleep tight!" she said, as she staggered out of the room and into her bedroom. Daniel knew there would be no taxi, his voices just switched off, as did the voices of Gloria's group, you could call them back on demand but they were only voices. His friends were real enough in conversation, but still… only voices.

Daniel watched a little television, then got ready for bed, washed, cleaned his teeth and put on pyjamas, went into his bedroom and closed the door. The night was particularly silent; Gloria was quiet and so were her voices; he soon, very quickly fell into a deep sleep.

Next morning Daniel woke up to daylight streaming into his room, he had overslept, what day is it? Monday, but it wasn't a school day, it was half term so there was no need to rush. He lay with his hands behind his head surveying the room. Something was different he thought. It was very quiet, very unusual; Gloria is always dropping things or banging crockery about in the kitchen. He threw his covers off and slipped on his dressing gown, after visiting the bathroom and having cleaned his teeth, he ventured into the kitchen – no Gloria? Funny he thought. She is usually on her second cup of tea by now. Daniel looked up at the kitchen clock, "good grief! It's gone ten" he said out loud. Had she gone out without waking him? He moved the curtain aside in the front room and looked out onto the front drive, no; the car was where she had left it the night before. "Hello!" he shouted in a loud voice. "Are you up Gloria? Are you awake?" There was still no answer, just silence. Daniel then ventured a tap on Gloria's bedroom door, nervously as first, but then having heard no reply he banged the door with a clenched fist. Still no response, and so he tried the door handle and slowly, very slowly, opened the door and peered in. Gloria was still in her bed, very still, so still that Daniel placed his hand on her, no movement; he walked around to the other side of her bed to see her face…

The eyes were wide open, starring at nothing, her mouth was also wide open, not breathing in, not breathing out, there was nothing. Gloria was dead. He put his hand on her face; it was cold, like meat from the fridge, no sign of any movement. "She must have died during the night" he said out loud. "What shall I do? Who do I have to call?"
Benji, his imaginary voice spoke, *'think, before you call anyone'* he said, *'think hard, the social services will*

be round here like a flash, removing you from the scene. Back into care...'

"You are so right Benji" answered Daniel. "I need to think hard about this situation."

'Don't you worry,' said the voice, *'I will help – don't rush anything, take your time!'*

Then the doorbell rang, and a very nervous puzzled Daniel answered the front door. A man in a yellow jacket and carrying a clip-board stood on the doorstep. "Hello young man, is your mother or father in?"

"No" said Daniel, "I live with my grandmother."

"Okay" said the man, "can I please speak to her then?"

"She's in bed" said Daniel, "err, got a very nasty cold."

"I see" said the man, "so no one is going to drive that lovely old car here?" he pointed his clip-board in the direction of the car in the drive... "Out onto the road today."

"No" said Daniel, shaking his head.

"Good" said the man at the door, "only we are going to dig a hole in the road, very close to your drive today, and we will have an automatic digger moving directly in front of your drive. So I'm afraid you and your poorly nan are going to be shut in, motor wise that is – today. It's a burst water pipe, but we will have fixed it and be gone by tomorrow. We will be as quick as that!"

"So will there be a big hole out in front of us" asked Daniel.

"Filled in, first thing in the morning, before you and your nan open your eyes" he said, tapping his clip-board, "all done and dusted as if we had never been!"

"I see" said Daniel, "thank you for warning us."

"All part of the service young man" said the man at the door as he turned and left, shouting "I hope your poorly nan is better tomorrow." He was quickly through the gate and vanished around the corner out of sight.

Daniel closed the front door and went back to his bedroom and hastily got himself dressed, made himself a cup of tea in the kitchen and put two slices of bread into the electric toaster. Then, just to make sure, he ventured back into Gloria's bedroom for a second look at his grandmothers body, making sure she was still dead! And dead she was! As a doornail!

"I'm not going back into care" said Daniel.

Quite right' said the voice of Benji his imaginary friend, *'we must somehow dispose of Gloria's body.'*

"You mean bury it ourselves?" queried Daniel "but how and where?"

'They are digging a hole right now, outside' said the voice.

"Yes, but there's workmen" said Daniel,

'*If I know workmen they will take a tea break, they are night workers*' said the voice of Benji. '*You must accept that you will get no sleep tonight, there is work to be done...*'
"Such as?" questioned Daniel.
'*First*' said the voice, '*we need to wrap Gloria's body in black bin bags from the garage, look for black tape or ties to keep the bags on the body. Get into old clothes, the darker the better because you don't want to be seen. We work tonight, late!*'

Daniel got the black bags and a large roll of black insulating tape from the garage, and set about covering and packaging poor Gloria, fortunately she was quite thin and small.

Night came, and the sound of workmen and machines continued into the early hours of the dark night, fortunately there was no moon... but there were arc lights. Daniel went out to the end of the drive as quietly as he could, so that he could get a good look at what was going on, and how many workmen there were, he counted three. The hole itself was long and narrow, and from where he stood without being seen, it looked very deep, perfect he thought. '*Perfect*' whispered the voice, '*couldn't be better.*'
"Yes, but what about the workmen?" whispered Daniel, "three of them!"
'*What's the time now?*' asked Benji, Daniel held his wrist high to catch the glow of the arc lights,

"Two o'clock" he said.

Any moment now' whispered Benji, *'those arc lights will go out and you will just have the low flashing warning lights, and the portable railings to stop anyone falling in in the dark, then the three thirsty men will drive off down to the all night cafe.'*

To Daniels amazement this is exactly what happened, just as Benji had said. The wheelbarrow hanging on the garage wall was used to transport the body of Gloria down the drive and up to the hole. *'All clear'* said the voice, *'first move the end of the rail aside, now, in one quick move, tip the body into the hole, NOW! Don't look around – tip it!'* Daniel tipped the barrow handles as high as he could and the packaged body slid into the hole – without a sound. *'Right, now put the railing back into position and let's get out of here'* said the voice. *'Perfect! Let's get back up the drive!'* Daniel hung the wheelbarrow back where it came from on the garage wall. *'Now go and get some sleep'* said Benji.

"But surely, they will see the body in the hole?" asked Daniel, "when they come back."

'No they won't' said the voice. *'Did you see that pile of earth rubble at the far end of the hole, ready for the cement lorry to arrive and tip it up before morning – that cement is quick setting, it will be solid by midday.'*

"Are you sure?" said Daniel.

'Positive!' said the voice.

Daniel threw himself on the bed in his bedroom without removing his clothes, and fell into a deep sleep.

He opened his eyes and turned his head in the direction of the noise of machinery coming from the end of the drive, he was still dressed lying on his bed – what time is it? He rolled off the bed and walked to the window, it was dawn, that half-light just before sunrise. The noise he could hear meant the men at the end of the driveway were still working – have they seen Gloria's body! Have they retrieved it? From inside that gaping black hole? He had to find out, even if it meant facing what he had done, he must know. He put on a jacket and left the house to face the workmen and confess his crime. As he reached the end of the drive, the workman that came to the door hours before – stood in front of him.
"Did we wake you young man?" he said, "I'm afraid our mini-digger is a noisy little devil, but we're nearly finished. As you can see." He pointed, "the hole is almost full."
Daniel almost sick with fear, looked at what was once a gaping cavern, it was no more than a patch of dirt as the mini-digger's bucket end fattened the surface, like a fist in a flower pot planting a pot of bulbs. "Amazing!" muttered Daniel, nervously, "you said you would finish by morning, and you did."

"Just a layer of cement with a skim of tar on top, and, Bob's your uncle" he said.
"Bob's your uncle" repeated Daniel with a nervous laugh.
'Bob's your uncle and granny is a plant' whispered the voice of Benji, *'you've done it, and I told you it was okay, well done Daniel.'*
"Not funny" said Daniel as he walked back up the drive, "I could have easily got caught disposing of poor Gloria's body like that."
'The alternative was you being taken back into care' said Benji; *'now you have a place all to yourself'* said the voice, *'pull yourself together!'*

Back in the house Daniel made a cup of tea, stupidly pouring two cups as if Gloria was about to walk in. He's right, I must pull myself together, and I've got to sort things out.

'Money' said the voice, *'you will need money, regular money, think about it!'*
"I will" answered Daniel. "Gloria's cash card and pin number for a start, everything is in that bureau desk of hers, in what she called the study."

Daniel found the card and the little black book where she kept what she called her reminders. She never could remember anything for more than ten minutes. It had pin numbers, telephone numbers, even her password for her computer. I'd forgotten she had a computer thought Daniel, it's a lap top, and it must be in her bedroom. She used to watch films on it at night in bed. He opened the door of her bedroom as he did the day before, slowly and nervously, as if she was still in there lying in her bed.

However, the bed was now empty with bedclothes thrown back and on the floor, as a result of wrapping the body up hastily into black plastic bags the night before. There was the computer, on the dressing table next to her jewellery box.
'Gold rings and necklaces' said the voice of Benji, *'gold is fetching a premium price at the moment…'*
Daniel cut in angrily, "I'm not a thief" he said, "I'll use her money out of necessity, but I'll not flog her jewellery."
'As you wish' said the voice, *'but you are a fool.'*
"I'm a fool for having dumped poor Gloria's body into a…" he hesitated, "into a bloody workman's hole! In an unmarked grave, never to be seen or heard of again!" he shouted!
'Shhhhh, now calm down' said Benji, *'you've got to stop panicking and think with a clear head; for instance, what do you say when people out there start asking where your grandmother is?'*
"She is sick in bed" answered Daniel.
'She can't be sick in bed forever, you are not thinking ahead' said the voice. *'Positive thinking is needed.'*
"Your right" said Daniel, "that part is going to be difficult. I can't say she's gone on holiday and left

295

me here alone, I'd have social services on my doorstep."

'We will think of something' said the voice, *'now, how are you going to get about? You can't drive that car, you can't get a licence, you're too young.'*

"When I get money from that hole in the wall at the bank, I can always get a taxi for shopping. Other than that I can use my bike. Now keep quiet, I'm going to use the computer."

First, the little black book, he thought, flicking through the pages, second the password of course. Now what could it be? It's got to be champagne! Gloria's favourite! The computer comes to life and Daniel enters her email address plus the password champagne... We are in, perfect!

"Just look at her emails, I didn't realise grandma had so many friends" said Daniel pointing.

'Most are probably dead' said Benji, *'she was a very old lady.'*

"Oops!" said Daniel, "not everybody, here is one coming in now..."

'Read it out loud' said the voice, *'I can't see it.'*

Daniel reads the incoming email...

What have you done with Gloria? We talk to her and as yet get no answer... Hamish and Dorothy.

"It can't be!" shouted Daniel, "it's her voices! They're emailing!"

'Don't answer' said Benji, 'it could be dangerous, the less they know the better.'

"But how?" said Daniel.

'Never mind how – just switch it off!' said the voice.

"They must know something" Daniel said worriedly, "do you think they know?"

'Switch it off!' repeated Benji, 'and close the lid…'

"But it's not possible" said Daniel, "you're just voices, you are not physical, how can they email? I'm scared they know something."

'It must be power of thought" said Benji, 'I can't think of any other way, mind over matter and all that stuff.'

"If they can send messages by thought, they can receive messages by thought. They either know something or they suspect" said a frightened Daniel.

'Stop worrying' said the voice, 'go and get some money from that hole in the wall, use your bicycle, you need money now! Go and get it!'

"You're right" Daniel said turning off the computer, "who was it who said money was the root of all evil? They were right, whoever they were."

'Stop whinging and go and get your bike and get some money' repeated the voice, 'NOW!'

Daniel checked his bike over in the garage, the front tire needed air again, and he pumped it up and promised himself that he would put it right by taking off the wheel and finding the slow leak in the tube and correcting it. Either that or buy a new tube. He checked that Gloria's cash card was safe in his pocket and that the pin number was in his pocket notebook, along with Gloria's 'just in case I forget notes!'

He knew the bank to go to because he often sat in the car keeping a lookout for meter wardens, while Gloria went into the bank, she would never use the hole in the wall, they were just for common people, with little money and no social standing in the bank, she had said, Gloria was a terrible snob.

On his arrival at the bank Daniel parked and chained his bike to the railings and made his way to the hole in the wall at the front of the bank, he glanced at his notebook, to check the pin number, before he got to the machine, then, placing the card in the slot he watched it disappear with anticipation. The voice of Benji told him *'don't ask for too large an amount, try two hundred and fifty, and ask for a receipt, it looks more professional.'*
Daniel entered the pin number and held his breath, he followed the written instructions and his [Gloria's], cash card reappeared, followed by a batch of crisp new notes, two hundred and fifty pounds, and then out popped a receipt. Sorted!

'Well done, I'm proud of you' said Benji.
"I'm not proud of myself" said Daniel, "and I never will be, as long as I live."

'Rubbish' said the voice, *'you will learn that life is all take, nobody gives in this modern day and age. Sad, but very true.'*

Daniel ignored his remarks and took off the safety chain and released his bike from the iron railings and headed through the busy traffic to the supermarket where Gloria was a regular. He must first look out for Eileen, who had introduced herself to him the day before, as being a friend of Gloria's and always keeping an eye out for his grandmothers' sake at the supermarket. As he was on a bicycle he was limited to what he could buy, breakfast cereal, a big container of milk, a chocolate bar and a cola, that will do for now. He found the till that Eileen was working and queued...
"Hi, you are Gloria's lad" she said.
"Grandson" said Daniel.
"Where is she today?" Eileen asked looking around.
"I'm afraid I had to leave her back at the house" lied Daniel, "she had a fall, the doctor thinks she may have sprained her ankle and must keep her weight off her foot. I'm on my bike today, but it looks as if I'll have to do the groceries for the next few weeks by taxi. Will it be okay for me to use her card? I'm paying cash today though.
Eileen said "it's best if you always use me and my till, I know the pin number and card are being used with her permission. So stick with me."

"Thank you so much, I'll tell her you were asking after her" lied Daniel, once again.

Eileen handed him two carrier bags with his goods and took his money. "We have to charge for plastic bags" she said, "so make sure you bring Gloria's shopping bags, she purchased them from here. Have a nice day!"

Daniel feeling very pleased with himself, left the store and headed for his bike...

"Hello, its Daniel isn't it?" said a voice from behind.

Daniel turned to see the tall figure of the social worker lady, from when he was first taken into care.

"My you've grown since I last saw you, quite the young man now" she said. "How is your grandmother?"

"She's okay" he stammered, "just resting today, so I'm doing the shopping."

"Well done" she said, "I must drop by soon and congratulate her on having such a fine young grandson."

"I must go" said Daniel nervously.

"Of course, mind how you go on that bike with two bags of shopping" she said, turning and left to go into the store.

A very worried Daniel hooked the heavy shopping bags, one each side of the handlebars, and rode out of the shopping centre and on to the main highway heading for home. Now what! Thought Daniel, if that social worker woman turns up at the front door, what do I say? I must get back and talk to Benji he thought, as his bicycle suddenly shuddered and the handlebars wobbled with the weight of the shopping bags. Daniel stiffened his legs, raising his bottom off the saddle as he looked down at the flat tyre shredding off the front wheel…

He never saw the truck that hit him full on, throwing the bicycle and the shopping into the air and poor Daniel under the huge wheels of the heavily laden truck. He was killed outright by the impact. It was the tarmac truck heading to top off the hole in front of his grandmother's house…

So now, dear reader, as this story comes to a close… I am now just a voice like all the other voices, but this time I am in YOUR head.

If you don't believe me, check your incoming emails on YOUR computer… It could even be the voice of Gloria!!!

The End

A little about the Author, Peter Maddocks, Fleet Street Cartoonist, and children's film maker, now resides in southern Spain. In 2011 he began to release his many 'How to draw books' in several different languages; Short stories for children, and a whole new collection of stories for adults, in eBook and paperback!

He spends a great deal of his time drawing, and painting in his many styles.

Please find examples of his work at:
petermaddocks.com

PublishedByMe.Blogspot.com

www.ingramcontent.com/pod-product-compliance
Lightning Source LLC
Chambersburg PA
CBHW070121090126
37978CB00030B/374